THOMAS DESTINY

JASON JAMES KING

JON GRUNDVIG

IMMORTAL WORKS

Salt Lake City

Immortal Works LLC
1505 Glenrose Drive
Salt Lake City, Utah 84104
Tel: (385) 202-0116

© 2016 Immortal Works
www.immortalworks.press

Cover Art by Carter Reid
http://www.thezombienation.com/

ISBN 978-0-692-78113-5 (paperback)
ISBN 978-1-5323-1827-6 (ebook)

For Samuel, I'm so proud of you now and always!

For Laura, always and forever.

1

THE LAST CAMP

My phone blared the invincibility star music from classic Mario Brothers, and I jerked my head up. I was lying on my stomach, just pulled out of an awesome dream where I was fighting three dragons with a singing sword while riding atop the back of a sarcastic, wise-cracking unicorn. Harriet Tubman was there too, for some reason, but she mostly supplied cover fire with her machine gun to keep the gargoyles off me so I could concentrate on killing the dragons. So my usual dream, basically.

My ringtone grew louder the longer I neglected my phone.

Why did I set my alarm? It's summer!

I let my head fall back down and covered it with a pillow while at the same time feeling around on the nightstand for my phone. My fingertips brushed it, and I was about to hit the home button to make the alarm snooze when reality slapped me across the face with the cold, raw chicken of remembering.

I set the alarm because I was going camping!

I rolled to get up, misjudging just how close to the edge of my bed I really was, and crashed to the floor in a tangle of sheets and blankets. My alarm music kept playing, which only fueled my excitement. I felt I could take on the world or at the very least stomp on the heads of malicious turtles that got in my way. I scrambled up, threw open my bedroom door, and darted across the hall to the bathroom.

"You ok, Thomas?" my mom called.

I would've answered, but my mouth was already full of toothpaste and spit. I pulled my t-shirt over my head, and it snagged on the toothbrush hanging out of my mouth. I managed to get it off and then spat into the sink—toothbrush and all.

"Thomas?"

"I'm fine!"

I hopped into the shower with one leg while trying to get my shorts off. I nearly slipped, and didn't succeed in undressing until after I'd cranked on the shower. I could still hear my phone playing the Mario star music, and I started humming along, and then making up my own lyrics.

I'm going camping today! I'm going camping today! Nah nah nah nah nah nah nah, I'm going camping with my friends today...

Ok, so I'd be a terrible song writer.

I slipped again as I leapt out of the tub, and only avoided falling by pulling on the towel hanging from the rack on the wall. Mom gasped as I threw open the bathroom door and bolted across the hall...wet and naked—the towel dangling from my hand.

I slammed my bedroom door and called, "Sorry."

On any other day I would've been embarrassed and horrified, but I was GOING CAMPING! So it didn't matter. I found a pair of jeans and a "clean-ish" t-shirt in my hamper and got dressed. I hummed the star music that still played on my phone, and didn't turn it off until I was ready to go to breakfast. That consisted of a marshmallow cereal poured into a drinking glass, with milk, and accidentally a bit of orange juice. I drank it down, nearly choking on a marshmallow red balloon, but not even that could stop me! I was invincible!

"Slow down," Mom warned when I nearly collided with her in the hallway to our living room.

"Sorry!" I said in between coughs, and then stepped around her.

She followed me into the room.

"Aren't you late for work?" I slid to a stop and examined the pile of gear I'd collected the night before. *Tent, sleeping bag, backpack, uniform, ten pounds of teriyaki flavored beef jerky*...I know ten pounds is a lot, even for a week-long trip, but you have to understand, I have a problem. I'm not proud of it, and someday I'll get it under control. Really, I can quit anytime I want.

"I told Phil I'd be in a little late so I could see you off."

"Aw, how sweet." I joked as I unzipped my pack and made one last check of my jerky store. I hoped it'd be enough for a week. Maybe I could buy some more at a gas station along the way.

"You have your phone?"

I wordlessly held it up for her to see as I re-zipped my pack.

"And your charger?"

"Yeah."

"And enough underwear?"

"Who needs underwear," I snorted.

I turned to catch a flat stare from Mom.

"Kidding!" I quickly said, and I mostly was.

"You have your first aid kit? And extra socks? And spare batteries for your flashlight?"

"Yes, Mom." I grabbed my rolled up sleeping bag and stood. "And my allergy medicine, and bug repellent, and sunscreen. Crap!"

"Hey!" she snapped. "What did I tell you about using that word?"

"It's not even a swear!"

"What did I say?" She repeated in that dangerous tone that always told me she meant business.

I rolled my eyes. "Substitute it with something better."

"Like?"

I shrugged. "I dunno. Crumpet! Mom, do we have to do this right now?"

"All right, all right! Just make sure you plug your phone into Brother Jackson's cigarette lighter every night."

"Mom, I'll be back on Friday," I said. "That's not even an actual week."

"I know." She forced a smile.

I dropped my sleeping bag next to the front door. "You weren't like this about the winter trek or spring hike."

"Those were only weekend trips. This is the longest we'll

have ever been apart." The tremor in her voice cooled my irritation, and I couldn't help but step up to her and wrap my arms around her.

"I'll be fine," I said in her ear before pulling away.

She nodded and wiped a tear off her cheek. "Look at you." She tilted her head up at me. "Already taller than me."

I chuckled. "Or maybe you're just really short."

She made a noise that was half sob, half laugh. "Well, I shouldn't be surprised. Your father was six-four."

That caught me off guard. It wasn't often that she spoke of my father. But when she did I ate it up, hungry for every detail. See, we didn't have any pictures of my dad. Mom had torn all of those up when he'd run off a month after I was born. So, other than what she'd tell me, I had no idea who he was or even what he looked like.

"He sure missed out on raising a wonderful son."

While I was always eager to hear about my dad, I never knew what to say when Mom talked about him. Did she want me to agree with her when she put him down? Was I supposed to hate him? I guess I did, but it was mixed with curiosity and a feeling of sadness.

A horn honk rescued me from the awkward moment, and I quickly kissed Mom on the cheek before bending down and grabbing my backpack. After I slung that over my shoulder, I snatched up my sleeping bag and was already out the door when she called her final goodbye. I just threw a wave behind me, not even bothering to turn around.

I wish I had.

My friend, C.J., threw open the door of Brother Jackson's

red extended cab pickup truck. "Throw your stuff in the back, Thomas!"

C.J. was a short, chubby kid with black curly hair. Pretty much the opposite of me physically, but we liked all the same stuff, so we could always be found together playing video games, or hanging out at Dr. Menace Comics.

"Where's your uniform, Thomas?" The middle-aged Brother Jackson asked from the driver's seat. I call him "Brother Jackson" because he was a volunteer from my church. That, and I'd never really bothered to learn his first name.

"In my pack." I waved to the truck bed where I'd deposited my things.

"Well as long as you brought it."

I absolutely *hated* wearing my scout uniform. Aside from the slacks being six inches too short and showing off my knobby ankles, it was hideous. Now, I'm not one to care much about fashion, but the uniforms the scout association made for young men were all an ugly mix of olive greens and tooth plaque yellows—like they'd been puked on by the nineteen seventies. I would wear it, but only when I absolutely had to. C.J. on the other hand loved wearing his uniform, and I suspected he had more than one. He said it made him feel like a soldier or something.

"Get in!" C.J. tugged on my shirt.

I climbed over C.J. to get into the truck. Another kid— whose name I didn't know—scooted over so I could sit in the middle. He was a big guy. Not just chubby, but big like a football player, and was at least a couple years older than me.

He had short blond hair and grinned in a way that made me think he might be special.

"I'm Bruno," he said with a wide grin.

I shared a look with C.J. and could tell he was thinking the same thing.

"I'm Thomas." I extended my hand.

He reached over and hugged me so hard that the breath left my lungs, and I found my face pressed up against Bruno's chubby chest. My head felt light and my vision turned into a black tunnel. I pictured my lifeless body lying on an examination table in the morgue, a doctor pronouncing my cause of death to be blubber asphyxiation.

"Everyone have their seatbelts on?" Brother Jackson called.

That made Bruno release me, and I desperately sucked in a lung full of oxygen.

Yup, this guy is definitely special.

Mom always told me to be nice to kids like Bruno, and I guess I wasn't mean to him. But I didn't include him in my conversations with C.J., even though he tried to break in a couple of times; usually talking about bizarre things he claimed to have eaten or wanted to eat. After not getting a response from us on what we thought giraffe might taste like, he finally got the hint and turned to stare out the window. I felt bad, but not bad enough to do anything about it.

It was late afternoon when we reached the Red Rock Canyon, giving us just enough time for some horsing around after we set up our tents. There were about a dozen boys at that camp, and only two leaders to keep us all under control— or at least from killing ourselves.

We hiked a bit out of the campsite, laughing and hassling one another along the way. Our rambunctious goofing around abruptly ended when Bruno belted out an obnoxious laugh at one of C.J.'s jokes. I hadn't noticed he'd followed us, and now everyone stared at him like he was a ghost.

"I'm Bruno." He held up half of an orange crayon. "The wrapper says it's supposed to taste like an orange, but I didn't think so. Wanna try?"

"Orange is the color, not the flavor," C.J. said.

"Then why do the commercials say they're fun *and* delicious?"

"They don't!" C.J. said.

After an awkward moment, the others resumed their friendly jibes and raucous conversations without any further response to the big kid. I watched Bruno's grin fade, cold guilt stabbing me in the chest. Still, I did nothing. He popped the rest of the crayon in his mouth, then turned and wandered back up the trail.

"Thomas!" C.J. called to get my attention. I spared one last look for Bruno, and then rejoined my friends.

Our rock throwing contest—the target being an old couple's camper down the next ridge—was cut short by Brother Jackson's call to dinner. And just in time too, because the last rock throw ended with the yelping of a dog, followed by angry shouting. We rushed back to camp and he made us put on our uniforms before we could eat, saying something about official scout business after dinner.

After we'd all grabbed our chicken and beans wrapped in tinfoil, he asked, "Where's Bruno?"

We exchanged looks with each other, and it was clear by

their confused expressions that the other boys didn't even know who Brother Jackson was talking about.

"He's probably just exploring," I said. "I'll go find him." I don't know why I volunteered, except that maybe I felt guilty for having excluded him.

I jogged up a rise and then down the trail we'd followed. "Bruno!" I called.

Sneaker prints led off the trail, big ones that obviously belonged to him, so I followed. After ten minutes I started to get nervous. While it wasn't dark, the sun was low, and I knew I didn't have a whole lot of time before it set. Also, there were cougars in this area, or at least that's what Mom said. Mountain lions were part of a list of dangers she made me memorize by repeating them over and over; a list that included rattlesnakes, scorpions, rabid coyotes, and creepy guys dressed as clowns. Well, I added that last part. She didn't think it was very funny.

I'd just decided to turn back when I heard water. I followed the sound to the base of a rock cliff where a waterfall made a pool. "Bruno?!" I shouted over the steady roar of the waterfall. "Bruno?!"

I let out an entirely too high-pitched scream when someone jumped from behind the waterfall and splashed down in the pool. Bruno waded toward me, laughing obnoxiously.

"That's not funny!" I snapped.

Bruno's smile faded, and he looked like he was going to cry.

"Ok, so maybe it was a little funny," I quickly said.

He grinned again and sloshed over to me.

"We gotta go, it's time for dinner! Real food, not... crayons, or giraffe." I started to walk, motioning for him to follow.

Bruno stood staring at me. "But he wants to meet you!"

I stopped, and turned back. "Who?"

"My friend!" Bruno grinned. "The man in the waterfall."

I stared at him for a moment and then forced a laugh. Bruno started laughing too, and then relief made my laughing real. "You got me, again."

"No, really! He's in the waterfall."

I stopped laughing. "Ok, stop it. You got me."

"Come meet him!" Bruno turned and sloshed back toward the waterfall.

"Dude! Come on! It'll be dark soon!"

Bruno didn't reply, but just climbed through the falling water and disappeared.

"Wonderful!" I hopped down into the pool. Surprisingly, the water was warm. Not hot like a hot tub, but warm and comfortable like that moment right after you pee in a swimming pool. Or, um...so I've heard, anyway.

I waded over to the waterfall, half expecting Bruno to jump out a second time for another scare, but he didn't.

"Ok, man," I shouted. "We gotta go!" I waited but he didn't answer. I leaned in closer to the waterfall. "Bruno?"

Nothing.

I stepped up on a rock and through the curtain of water, slipping and stumbling forward into a tunnel that I hadn't known was there. I quickly scrambled up and looked around. Blue glowing moss on the walls and floor lit the cave enough for me to see a few feet ahead. I leaned down and touched the moss, and my fingertips came away glowing blue. I'd read about this kind of thing in science class, but the book said this stuff was exotic and grew in weird, faraway countries—like Canada.

"Thomas!" Bruno stepped out of the darkness. "Come on!" He waved for me to follow.

I looked back at the curtain of water behind me, and said, "This is awesome, but I think we should come back tomorrow, when it's daytime."

Bruno didn't even hear me. He just kept walking until he disappeared into the darkness. "Bruno!" I shouted, and then jogged after him. I followed a bend in the tunnel and found him standing in front of a wall giggling. That's when I noticed that it wasn't a wall, but some kind of metal door.

In the dim light of the blue glowing moss, the metal's rusty surface had made it blend in with the red rock cave, but the handle and three open slits near the top of the door gave it away. There was also writing inscribed in the metal from a language I didn't know. "Is that Chinese?" I asked, and immediately felt stupid as anyone with a fourth grade education could tell that it wasn't.

Bruno turned to look at me. "Thomas, this is Ajii! He's my friend!"

"Your friend is a creepy metal door?"

Ok, so I thought the kid was probably lonely and all, but come on! All *my* imaginary friends at least had been something cool, like Ninja Hamster Hiroto, or my dinosaur pal with red eyebeams, Lasersaurus, not Dori the Rusted Metal Door...

Bruno just laughed. "No, silly! Ajii's inside!"

So clearly Bruno was more than a little special, he was also crazy. That's what I thought as I stared into the blackness beyond the slits in the metal door. "Ok, Bruno. I've met Ajii, so now it's time to..."

Eyes appeared from within the darkness, and I am not ashamed to tell you that I peed myself a little—and by a little, I mean a lot. "Someone's in there!"

Hello Thomas, a high pitched voice said. But the really freaky thing was that it didn't say it out loud, but inside my head. *I'm Ajii.*

I couldn't speak. I couldn't run. I just stood there staring stupidly at those round, pale green eyes—eyes that had no irises or pupils. "What are you?" I squeaked out.

I'm trapped.

"He needs our help, Thomas," Bruno said. "That's why he wanted to meet you."

"W-we'll go for help," I stammered. "Brother Jackson can call search and rescue and..."

No, only you can help me.

"Why?" My voice cracked again, because of fear, not puberty...I promise.

You have the ability. I could sense you coming for miles.

"Um, ability?"

Yes, a very rare thing among the people here. But it isn't natural with you. You have cords tethering you to a greater power.

"What?"

Touch the runes on my door and I will tell you what to say.

"Look, I think we should go."

No! Ajii screeched in my head, something that nearly knocked me to the ground. *Please,* he said in a gentler tone. *Please don't leave me. I've been in here so long!*

Questions I probably should've asked Ajii at that moment: Why are you trapped? Who put you in there? And are you evil? In hindsight, I guess the chances of him answering honestly were probably pretty slim. In any case, I was too shocked and terrified to think clearly. I just wanted to get out, but that terrible, high-pitched voice drilled into my brain, and wouldn't let me leave. Not unless I did what it wanted.

I stretched out my hand and touched the strange lettering on the metal door.

Good! Good! Ajji squealed in delight. *Now repeat the following words.*

I spoke them the moment they entered my mind, and it felt less like repeating and more like I was a puppet and Ajii the ventriloquist. "Bakara. Seimakasha. Baksyroc." Bruno giggled at the strange words, and I couldn't help but wonder how he wasn't scared out of his mind like I was. "Une shei shei," I finished.

The letters on the door lit up, some glowing white, some red, and some green. Then they started to shift and rearrange themselves. I couldn't believe what I was seeing. It was like something out of Harry Potter. The letters finally settled into a new pattern and turned blue, the same color as the luminescent moss. Then the glow of the letters faded and an eerie silence fell over the cave. It was like someone pressed the mute button on the world. I couldn't hear anything; not my breathing, not the echoes of the cave, not even the dull roar of the waterfall behind us.

"Ajii?" I asked.

Terrible laughing, high-pitched and wild filled my mind, and the cave started to shake. Rocks and dirt fell from above, and every instinct told me to run. I grabbed Bruno by the arm and pulled him back toward the mouth of the cave. His smile was gone now, replaced with a look of terror that mirrored my own. The shaking got worse, and I tripped. Bruno pulled me up and we leapt through the waterfall and landed in the pool with a big splash.

A thick beam of light, like a spotlight, exploded from the cave along with a spray of rocks and dirt. A fist-sized chunk that was more rock than dirt hit me in the head, and the last thing I remember was hearing Bruno say, "I think we did something bad."

Then everything went dark.

2
THE GUARDIAN

I woke up just as Bruno was leaning over me, mouth open as he moved in to kiss me. Well, not really *kiss* as much as start rescue breathing, but at that moment they really seemed like the same thing.

I pushed on his face. "I'm ok!"

Bruno fought me, still trying to place his mouth over mine. "But Brother Jackson said this is what we're supposed to do when someone drowns."

"I'm not drowned!" I screamed.

"Oh," Bruno said, and he rocked back onto his legs.

I sat up as quick as I could, noticing that indeed I was sopping wet. I remembered jumping into the pool, but the water had only come up to my waist. Why was my hair wet? I brushed soggy brown strands out of my eyes and stopped as my fingers brushed a bump on my forehead. I pulled my hand away to find pink, diluted blood on my fingertips.

"A rock hit you in the head, and you fell into the water," Bruno said. "I saved you!"

I eyed the big kid warily before nodding my head. "Thanks."

"Ajii got out," Bruno said. "I think he might be bad."

I looked toward where the waterfall had been. The entire cliff face was cracked, broken and marred by a gaping hole in the rock. "Which way did he go?"

Bruno pointed in the direction of our camp.

My chest got tight and I blurted out, "C.J.!"

Bruno helped me stand, and we started running back through the trees toward the hiking trail. Bruno had a hard time keeping up, but I didn't slow to make it easy for him. A monster— worse than any wild predator Mom worried about —had escaped, and it was headed toward my best friend and the rest of my group. I wasn't sure exactly what it was that Ajii wanted, or what he would do to the others, but a sick feeling in my gut told me he wouldn't just ignore them.

As we descended the hill leading back into camp, I caught sight of the ring of tents we'd set up, only now they were collapsed and torn. Mine was shriveled, black, and smoking like it'd been burned down. The fire pit smoldered, our propane grill lay on the ground, and a squirrel picked through the food spilling out of an overturned cooler. The ruined camp was completely empty of people.

While running toward the pickup truck to see if anyone was hiding inside, I tripped on a rock. I caught myself before falling, and glanced down at the chunk of stone. It wasn't a normal rock you'd find lying around nature, but a piece of marble like what statues were made of. I picked it up and found half of a face etched into one side of it. This *had* come from a statue. Other pieces of marble were scattered all around the campsite. Some were large and looked to be torsos and legs, and some were small like heads or hands. It was like someone had gone wild inside an art museum with a sledge hammer.

"Hey this one looks like Brother Jackson!" Bruno said as he held up a marble head.

"No," I choked out. "No!" I said again as I frantically began grabbing marble pieces and examining the faces etched into each of the heads. I knew these faces, especially the one of the kid with curly hair and glasses. "C.J." I sat down on the ground and just stared at what was left of my best friend.

Tears came a few minutes later, and I didn't stop crying until long after the sun went down. Ajii had turned my friends into statues, and then in an extra act of cruelty, had smashed them to pieces. And *I* was the one that let him loose.

Bruno sat next to me, and to my surprise, didn't shed any tears. He was handling this nightmare with far more bravery than I was.

"This is my fault," I sobbed.

Bruno patted my back, but didn't say anything. What could he say? It was true. My best friend and a dozen other innocent people were dead because of me. Their families would never see them again, and would probably never even know what happened.

"You just going to sit there and cry all night, kid?" a deep voice startled me. I whipped around to see the outline of a man standing only a few feet away. From what I could tell, he was unusually tall, and wore a long coat, like a cowboy's duster. His other features were shadowed by the night, but my fear faded when I realized it wasn't Ajii.

"Who are you?" I sniffed and wiped my runny nose on my arm.

The man stepped closer and I could see that he was older, probably late forties, with messy brown hair and several days' worth of stubble lining his jaw and chin. "I was going to ask if you realize what it is you unleashed, but it looks like you already get it."

I nodded. "A monster." Then the tears started again.

The man stared down at me and his scowl faded. "I'm sorry for your loss. I really am."

I leaned my forehead against C.J.'s marble forehead and sobbed.

"My name is Lobo, and I'm a guardian," the man said.

"Ooooh! A real life guardian!" Bruno exclaimed. "Can you sign my armpit?" He started to pull up his shirt.

Lobo seemed to notice Bruno for the first time. "Do you even know what a guardian is?"

"No," Bruno said.

Lobo stared at the big kid for a long moment and then groaned. "Oh no... I know what you are."

"I'm Bruno!"

"Right," Lobo said with a deep sigh.

"What's a guardian?" I asked with another sniffle.

"The short answer?" Lobo exhaled. "I fight Dreja—creatures like the one you released."

I put C.J.'s marble head down. "He said his name was Ajii."

Lobo nodded. "That one's a very powerful, very dangerous Dreja."

"What's a Dreja?" I asked, my tears finally stopping.

"Creatures twisted by dark forces. They trade their sanity for enhanced bodies or arcane power."

"Arcane power? Like magic?" I tried to sound skeptical because I didn't want to believe what just happened, but I couldn't deny what I'd seen or the dead friends scattered all around the campsite.

"Magic, science, miracles," Lobo said. "Call it what you will, but what it really boils down to is knowledge. Know how to do something, and you can do it. Even if that something is teleportation, calling lightning, or controlling fire. You humans already do seemingly miraculous things. Your ancestors would probably call airplanes, cars, or computers magic, but to you it's just an application of greater knowledge."

"*You humans?*" I asked. "You're not human?"

Lobo shook his head. "I'm not from your world."

"Then where are you..."

"Look, we don't have time to play twenty questions," Lobo said cutting me off.

"Animal, mineral, or chicken?" Bruno said and then he started laughing. "I bet it's chicken!"

Lobo rolled his eyes and then said to me, "If we don't do something to stop Ajii, a lot more people are going to die."

That made me want to start crying again, but I fought back the tears. "What do you mean, *we?*"

Lobo took a deep breath. "I need your help."

"I don't know how to fight monsters!"

"You let him out, so you need to be the one to put him back. It's the way the magic of his prison works. Failing that I'll need to kill him, which I'm not sure I'm strong enough to do alone." Lobo stared at me for a long moment before finally asking, "Do you want to avenge your friends and set things right?"

"Yeah, but..."

"Then we need to get moving. Ajii's likely fifty miles from here by now." Lobo started walking away from what was left of the camp.

I stood up. "Where's Ajii going?"

"To open a gate to another world and summon more of his kind," Lobo called back.

"Do you have a phone?" I shouted. "I need to call my mom, and mine's toast." I looked at what was left of my tent.

"Sorry, kid. I don't use your technologies—they cause cancer."

I hurried after Lobo, falling in beside him and then glancing back at Bruno who was trundling after us. "But shouldn't we call for help or something?"

"We *are* the help," Lobo said.

"And Bruno?"

"Well we can't leave him here." Lobo glanced at the big kid. "He might eat something endangered," he added under his breath.

"What?" Bruno shouted from several feet behind.

I shook my head. "I don't understand!"

Lobo chuckled. "There's a lot you don't understand, kid. I'll do my best to give you a crash-course while we travel."

"A crash-course in what?" I asked.

3

THE TRUE WAY OF THINGS

We climbed into the cab of a rusty, beat-up old truck that was probably older than my grandma. And just like grandma, it smelled of old cigarettes and gasoline.

Bruno wrinkled his nose. "This truck smells icky." He licked the window. "Tastes funny, too."

"Guess being a guardian doesn't pay much, does it?" I tried to roll down the window, but the crank wouldn't budge.

"This vehicle will get us where we need to go." Lobo turned the key, and the engine struggled for a second before roaring to life.

"And where is that?"

"Las Vegas, Nevada!" Lobo said as he shifted the truck into gear and pulled onto a gravel road.

"Does Ajii have a beat up piece of crap truck too?"

"He can fly."

"And I'm guessing he's not going to Vegas to play the slots?"

Lobo looked at me and smiled. "You're a sarcastic little juvenile, aren't you?"

I shied away from his intimidating stare. "Sorry."

"Don't be." He chuckled and shifted the truck into a higher gear. "To answer your question, there's a weak spot in the fabric of space-time in Vegas; something to do with all the brightly colored artificial lighting and constant use of electric power. Ajii's not at his full strength yet, but when he is, he'll be able to tear open a portal to another world."

Great. I decided then and there that I was never going to sleep with my nightlight on again, not if it meant it made it possible for a trans-dimensional demon to rip its way into our reality. Not that I sleep with a nightlight...I mean, I'm twelve after all. I gave that up weeks ago.

"Is that how you got here?" I asked.

Lobo shifted again and the truck jerked. Bruno's head hit the ceiling of the cab, and he whimpered and started rubbing it.

"I did something similar," Lobo said. "But most who travel the realms use a bridge. It's a kind of permanent hole in space-time that joins two worlds together. They're common in the cosmos, and most planets have several. In fact, there's a network of bridges that intersect in a world called The Crossroads, a place where beings from across the galaxy pass through on their way to other planets."

I scoffed. "Throw in a bunch of panhandling hobos, and that sounds like an intergalactic bus station."

Lobo shot me another weird smile, one that looked proud for some reason. Like I'd just won a spelling bee even after being given the word *Chiaroscurist.* Fun fact, that means an artist who specializes in light and shadow techniques. I know that because that's the word that lost our school champion the state spelling bee. I competed too, but was out in the first round after misspelling *toilet*.

"So how did you know Ajii escaped?"

Lobo shifted gears again and shot a glance at me. "You want the long answer or the short answer?"

"I just want answers!" I snapped, and I could feel the tears threatening again.

"You help me stop Ajii, and I'll give you all the answers you can handle."

I ran a hand through my hair. "I can't believe this is really happening."

"Sooner or later we all have to face the true way of things."

"Thanks for the comfort," I said dryly. "You sure you didn't miss your true calling as a therapist?"

Lobo sighed. "I know it's a lot to take in so suddenly. I'm really sorry."

Sorry? Why was Lobo apologizing to *me*? I'd been the one to free Ajii and cause the deaths of my best friend and scout troop. I'd caused this nightmare because I was too cowardly to follow my conscience. I turned to stare out the window as if we were passing the most amazing scenery, though it was near total blackness outside. I just didn't want Lobo to see me crying.

The urgency and excitement faded as the truck ate up mile after mile of lonely canyon road, and I began to get very tired. Bruno was already asleep by the time we reached the interstate, and was leaning his head on my shoulder and drooling on my arm. I asked Lobo a few more questions, but the lateness of the hour and emotional drain of the day's events got to me, and my eyelids drooped.

When I woke up, we were already in Vegas, and I was surprised that I'd slept so soundly in the rickety, funny smelling cab of the old truck. Lobo handed me a sack full of breakfast sandwiches wrapped in yellow paper. He was eagerly eating one, and looked to be enjoying it like it was made of pure sunshine and happiness.

"Earth has *the best* food!" he announced when he finally finished his egg, bacon, sausage, and cheese muffin. "I love your drive-thrus. Nothing like them anywhere else in the cosmos!"

"And you're worried about phones giving you cancer?" I muttered. "Guess you don't know about heart disease."

He took a pull on the straw of a thirty-two-ounce soda and then burped. "And I love this pepper drink."

"Or diabetes."

I noticed Bruno wasn't sitting next to me. I was about to ask where he was when the whole truck rocked. Lobo let go of the shifter and pounded on the cab's rear window. "I said stop that!" he shouted.

I turned to see Bruno standing upright in the bed of the pickup. He was jumping up and down like he was on a trampoline. Lobo quickly rolled down the driver's side window and roared, "HEY!"

Bruno froze, looked at us through the cab window, and then plopped down on one of the truck's wheel well covers. His mouth turned down in a sullen expression, and he kicked an empty fast-food sack up in the air so that it caught the wind and flew down the road behind us.

"Aren't you worried he's going to fall out?" I asked while watching Bruno sway with the moving of the truck.

"He already has." Lobo fished in the white sack and pulled out another breakfast sandwich. "Twice."

I stared at Bruno through the window, looking for road rash or other signs of injury. He didn't have any scratches or bruising. The only things I could see that would indicate he'd fallen out of a truck at high speed were the small holes torn into his scout uniform.

That reminded me of what Lobo said earlier. "Back at camp, you said you knew what Bruno was. What did you mean?"

Lobo glanced at Bruno in the rearview mirror. "He's not human. He's a Gigas; a nearly extinct race of giants from a world that no longer exists."

I glanced back through the cab window and caught Bruno picking his nose with his index finger. "He's a little on the chubby side, but he really isn't *that* big for a fourteen-year-old." Bruno stuck that same finger in his mouth and I looked away with a shudder.

"That's because he's a *baby* Gigas."

"Baby?" Suddenly Bruno's comments and odd behavior started to make sense. Well not make sense. What Bruno does, says, and eats still doesn't make sense, but I understood then that he wasn't special, not in the way I'd been thinking. He acted like a little kid because he *was* a little kid.

Lobo nodded. "He may be fourteen, but for his race, that's probably equivalent to five human years. I'm surprised to find one here of all places, and I couldn't begin to guess who brought him to Earth. But they probably did it to protect him. See, the Gigas were once renowned warriors. That's why they were hunted to near extinction and their planet..."

Sirens cut off Lobo's explanation—lots of sirens. More than I'd ever heard at once.

"He's already here!" Lobo said dropping his half eaten egg muffin on the bench.

I looked out the window and found we were coming off the freeway in the middle of what could only be downtown Las Vegas. I hadn't ever been there before, so I wasn't sure what to expect. From the way Mom always talked about it, I thought the entire city would be made out of flashing neon lights and have pinball flippers in place of stop signs. But that's not the way it was. Aside from some tall buildings on the Strip that were obviously casinos, Las Vegas wasn't all that different from other cities.

A few minutes later we had to abandon the truck as we weren't allowed on the Strip. A police barricade was set up there, and a crowd of people anxiously chattered and shouted questions at the officers. A dozen or so police cars were parked outside the front of a building called Caesar's Palace along with some ambulances. There was even a reporter holding her microphone and talking to a camera.

Lobo led us away from the crowd, and we were able to sneak in through an enormous parking garage. I'm not sure exactly how Lobo knew where to go, or how to avoid being caught, so I chalked it up to him being a "guardian"— whatever that meant.

Once inside, we were greeted by a scene that made me

choke back a sob. It was like seeing my ruined camp all over again, except this time there were whole people statues as well as broken pieces of marble. One guy was even still sitting at a flashing slot machine, his marble hand clutching the pull lever.

Lobo stopped us and glanced around warily. Then he said in a hushed tone, "You're going to need a weapon." He pulled from within his coat a long, glass wand. Well it looked like it was made of glass, but it was probably magic crystal or something because it was heavy and felt like metal.

Lobo offered the handle of the wand to me and said, "This wand will shoot lightning where you point it when you say the magic word."

"What's the magic word?" I asked, hesitant to touch the wand.

He glanced around the casino before turning back to me and answering, "Jackpot."

"Did you just make that up?"

Lobo frowned. "No..."

I glanced at the side of a slot machine behind me. Along its top, in flashing digital letters blinked the word "Jackpot."

"Yes *you* did!"

"Fine!" Lobo rolled his eyes. "There is no *magic word* to activate the wand! You just need something to focus your will to control its power. Saying *Jackpot* will do that."

I took the wand. "You could've picked a command that was more magical, like maybe a Latin word or something," I grumbled.

"No fair! *I* want a wand!" Bruno yelled.

Lobo hissed as he covered Bruno's mouth. They locked

eyes, and when Bruno nodded, Lobo drew back his hand. "Quiet!" he said through clenched teeth.

"Ok!" Bruno shouted.

Lobo sighed and pulled a marble sized ball of silver metal from his trench-coat pocket. "Giving this to you is probably about as safe as teaching a toddler a fire spell, but we're desperate."

He handed the bead to Bruno who took it and stared at it with a disappointed frown. He opened his mouth to speak—or to eat it, I'm not entirely sure—but cut off when the bead melted into his palm and disappeared. Bruno closed his hand and giggled. "That tickles."

"What..." I started, but then a silver club materialized before Bruno, the handle already fitted into his grip.

"That magic bead melts into a person's body, then chooses what weapon is best suited for them and creates it whenever they need it."

Bruno looked a little too excited as he swung the club in the air to test it and his innocent giggle turned into a disturbing, dark chuckle.

I was about to ask Lobo where *his* weapon was when a flash of blue light exploded from his hand, leaving in its place a beautiful silver sword with jewels embedded in the cross-guard and bottom of the handle. The blade glowed with a soft blue aura and I swear I could hear it hum whenever Lobo moved it.

"Now, Thomas, I need you to be brave like your favorite deity."

"My favorite deity? You mean like a god?"

"Yes. I was once a serious student of your illustrated holy

books, and I know Earth has an entire pantheon of patron deities and that everyone has their favorite. Mine is the man who turns green when he gets angry, or the one that can climb walls like a spider."

"Are you talking about super heroes?" I laughed more out of surprise than because it was funny.

Lobo didn't respond to me, but instead chewed his lip as he warily glanced around the casino. "Opening a rift in space-time takes a lot of magic. So, Ajii will probably be focusing all of his power on that spell."

"So, what does that mean?" I asked.

"That means," Lobo said, still not looking at me, "that we probably don't have to worry about him turning us to stone or attacking us with other spells."

"Well, that's good," I said, trying to keep my voice from trembling.

Lobo looked at me. "Ready?"

"I guess," I said, trying to fight back another wave of tears.

"The plan is for me to subdue Ajii, and when I have him held, I will call out the spell for returning him to his prison. Just repeat the words I say. That's all you have to do. Got it?"

I nodded, gripping the handle of the crystal wand so tight that it should've broke in my hand.

"These weapons are just for your own defense in case things go wrong. Don't attack Ajii unless I tell you to."

"Aw, but I wanna break stuff!" Bruno whined.

"Let's go!" Lobo said, and then he was moving.

4

STONE AND TEARS

We wove through rows of slot machines, and then entered an area that looked like an indoor mall. The building was deserted; the only signs of people the broken chunks of stone scattered across the floor. I tried not to look at the marble faces staring blankly at me. This was my fault. I wasn't sure how I would be able to live with that, but I guess at the moment I was more concerned with just living.

We descended a ramp and entered a gigantic open area decorated like some ancient coliseum. There were statues made of plaster all over the room, some of mermaids, some of muscular men with their arms outstretched. The domed ceiling was painted to look like the sky, clever lighting making it look almost real. There was a fountain that reminded me of an elf city in Lord of the Rings, and standing in the center of the coliseum was a tall figure.

I finally got my first real look at Ajii. Like I said, he was tall, real tall—like eight feet tall. He was facing away from us, his spine visible through his hunched back, and his skin was a sickly grey color. His arms were so long that his clawed hands reached below his knees.

It's the boy with the magic he doesn't know he has, Ajii said inside my head. I saw both Lobo and Bruno wince, so I knew they heard his high-pitched voice too. *And he's brought a new friend!*

"I am Lobo! A guardian and hunter of Dreja! You will submit to being returned to your prison, or you will be destroyed!"

Ugly, cackling laughter filled my head, and Ajii turned around. I gasped when I saw that he had no nose or mouth. Save for two eye holes, his whole head was a smooth, white ball on top of a grotesquely thin neck. It didn't match the color of his skin, so it must've been some kind of mask, and I really didn't want to know what Ajii looked like underneath.

It took seven of your kind to bind me the first time, and you think that just one of you and two Earth children can stop me now?

"Last chance, Dreja!" Lobo shouted. "I know you're not yet at your full strength! Submit or die!"

I won't need my full strength! More horrible laughter. It was giving me a headache.

Ajii raised his clawed hands and something rippled through the air. I felt it more than saw anything, and for a moment it seemed that nothing would happen. Then the statues decorating the coliseum began to move. The muscular men, a couple of centaurs, and even the mermaid broke loose from their pedestals and began moving toward us. Apparently, Ajii *could* still attack with magic.

I saw the surprise and panic on Lobo's face. "Protect him!" he shouted.

At first I thought he was talking to me, but then I realized he'd been shouting at Bruno. The big boy nodded sharply, a serious look on his face that I hadn't seen before. Lobo launched himself at Ajii, leaping into the air in an inhuman arc that would make any NBA power forward weep with envy.

A loud crack and an explosion of dust drew my attention away from Lobo, and I saw Bruno tear through one of the centaur statues with his baseball bat-like club. I heard heavy footfalls behind me, and spun to see the statue of a bearded muscular man clomping my way. I raised the glass wand, aimed it, and screamed "Jackpot!"

A bolt of blue electricity arced from the tip of the wand and struck at the muscled chest of the statue—probably some Roman god I should know the name of. It exploded into a million pieces, and I had to shield my face to avoid getting plaster dust in my eyes. Bruno continued bashing living statues into broken chunks, each time yelling out what I think were supposed to be action hero lines like, "Knock Knock, who's there? SMASH GORDON!" Or "What's black, white, and red all over? DIE THAT'S WHAT!" That second one wasn't half bad.

I used the lightning wand to send bolts of destruction everywhere I saw statues moving, taking out three really big ones...and one innocent window mannequin. I gotta admit, it was kinda cool, and it started to make me feel like I could hold my own in the fight.

When all of the walking statues were destroyed, I turned

back to watch Lobo fighting Ajii. It *was* like something out of a comic book or super hero movie. Ajii moved incredibly fast, swinging the clawed hands at the end of his thin ape-like arms at Lobo, who repeatedly ducked, dodged or blocked with his glowing sword. This continued for what felt like a long time, but probably was only a minute, and then the two finally broke apart, Lobo's shoulders heaving as he held his sword up in front of him.

Ajii didn't look winded like Lobo, but then again, I wasn't sure how to tell. I couldn't see his face, and his twisted grey body didn't appear to sweat. I did notice he had a red gash in his side, so Lobo had struck the monster at least once. Score one for the good guys!

Lobo charged Ajii again, actually lopping off one of the creature's rising hands. This time Ajii cried out, not telepathically but with a muffled voice from behind his mask. It was more of an animal screech than the pained yell of a person, and hearing it made me shake inside.

Lobo spun around so he was behind Ajii, and brought his sword up to the front of the Dreja's skinny grey neck. Ajii froze, gripping his bleeding stump. "Now, Thomas!" Lobo shouted. "Gorak, Tyrik, Shundam, Halithia!"

"Gorak," I began, but trailed off as Ajii threw out his remaining hand so it pointed at me.

A red blast of magic shot from Ajii's open palm, and I stood helpless, just watching like an idiot as the light streak toward me. Lobo released Ajii and exploded into a run, moving so fast that his form blurred. I shut my eyes and turned my head, expecting to die or be turned into a statue, but nothing happened. When I opened my eyes, I found

Lobo standing between me and Ajii. He glanced over his shoulder at me, and his sword clanged to the floor.

"Lobo?" I blurted out.

He met my stare, then fell.

All of my first aid training flooded into my mind, but I couldn't find any visible wounds on Lobo's chest. I actually laughed at myself. First aid for being blasted by magical power? What was I thinking? All I could do was catch Lobo and ease him to the ground.

Ajii's horrible cackling filled my head, making my brain hurt. He said nothing, but returned to meditating, or casting a spell, or whatever it was he was doing to open the rift.

Lobo looked up at me, a trickle of blood running out of his nose. His mouth worked like a fish out of water, trying to form words, but nothing came out. Finally, he was able to wheeze, "You're so tall."

And then his body turned to stone right before my eyes and began to crumble into chunks. Tears rolled down my cheeks. At first I thought they were from panic, but my fear was actually gone. My tears were from grief, which quickly turned into white hot anger.

I looked up to where Ajii stood in the center of the plaster coliseum. He had both arms—one of them ending in a bloody stump—raised above his head. Translucent waves of power pulsed from him in increasing intervals. I stood, stepping over Lobo's body and strode forward, my magic wand held out in front of me. I was surprised to find Bruno walking at my side, his liquid metal club held tightly in his hand.

"Hey!" I screamed at Ajii.

The Dreja didn't look until I had shouted a second time. *Don't pester me right now, boy!* he said as he turned his back to me. *I'm busy!*

I responded by shouting, "Jackpot!" A blue bolt of electric power shot out of my wand and struck the Dreja in the back. But to my horror, Ajii only flinched.

The monster turned, eye-holes changing from a pale green to an angry red. I yelled, "Jackpot!" again, and another lightning bolt exploded from the glass wand and struck Ajii in the chest. He shuddered, but showed no other signs of pain or injury. Fear returned, putting my anger out like water on a fire.

I was going to keep you alive so you could take me to it! Ajii's high-pitched voice drilled into my mind. *But now, I think I'm just going to kill you.*

In a blur of grey, Ajii streaked toward me, remaining claw raised to strike. He brought it down, but Bruno knocked it aside with his silver club.

Bruno had an angry scowl on his face, a look that was almost as frightening as Ajii himself. I didn't have time to thank him, because Ajii was already swinging for us again. Bruno batted the monster's claw away from him with a backswing of his club, and shoved me to the side so hard that I fell to the ground. I rolled, but quickly rose to my knees.

Bruno was stronger than I would've given him credit for. I guess even baby Gigases were tough. He knocked Ajii's attacks aside with ease, but the Dreja was faster, and had already managed to rake Bruno's stomach and upper arm with its razor claws. Bruno fought hard, but it was clear that Ajii was going to overpower him.

The hot anger in my chest came back, and I found the crystal wand on the ground, scooped it up and climbed to my feet. I didn't shoot at Ajii this time, but instead ran at the monster. It had knocked Bruno's club away, making it vanish, and kicked the big kid to the ground. Ajii raised a claw to finish Bruno when I crashed into him. We both went down, rolled, and came to a stop where I found myself sitting on top of the monster's chest.

Something really weird happened then. A vision flashed across my mind. It was like a black and white video of me sitting on top of Ajii, like someone was recording the whole fight with their phone from ten feet away. I saw exactly what Ajii was going to do, and saw what I should do to stop him. It wasn't just an idea that came into my mind, but an actual scene playing out like a movie. Then it ended, sending me back to the moment. I looked down at Ajii. The Dreja's muscles tensed and he began lifting his claw. So, I did what I'd seen myself do in the vision.

I jammed the point of the crystal wand into Ajii's right eye-hole and screamed, "JACKPOT!"

AJii's head exploded, shooting brain and bits of white mask in all directions. The force of the blast was so strong that it threw me off of the Dreja, and shattered the crystal wand. I rolled a few feet away, and hadn't even risen to my knees when a large hole appeared above Ajii's headless body. I'm not sure "hole" is the best way to describe it, because it looked more like a giant had punctured a nail through the air itself. An invisible force yanked me toward the hole. I tried to stop myself by clawing at the floor, but the suction was too strong. I realized what was happening right before the rift pulled us in.

5

FALLING OUT

The Crossroads was stranger than I'd imagined. I guess I really had started to think it'd be an alien bus station. Instead, it was a planet a lot like Earth with only two major differences: First, it was always night; the cloudless sky looking like the star show at the planetarium. Second, the entire place, except for the one and only city, was a junkyard of stuff from all over the universe. Alien vehicles, farming equipment, refrigerators, an old pirate ship, and mountains of junk from a hundred worlds littered the ground in every direction as far as I could see.

We walked for hours, but because the sky was always dark, I had no idea what time it was—though it felt like bedtime. Bruno and I found what looked to be some kind of transport vehicle, like a giant space semitrailer. We climbed inside—staying near the doors for fear of what might be lurking further inside the transport—and I tried to go to sleep.

You'd think after a day that was draining for both body and mind, and being on the planet of eternal night, it would've been easy to fall asleep—nope. I shifted and turned trying to get comfortable. Bruno didn't seem to have any problems nodding off. Just as soon as we'd climbed inside the storage vehicle, he rocked forward onto his face and fell asleep with his butt in the air; his snoring loud and constant like the sound of a lawnmower.

Every time *I* closed my eyes and started to drift, I saw C.J.'s marble face in my mind, and then Lobo's. They had died because I was a coward and let Ajii out of his cage. That's why I'd done it. I wasn't like Bruno who thought we were saving him. I knew Ajii was dangerous—deep down anyway—but I ignored my gut and let him out, and dozens of people had paid the price. Perhaps to live out my life far from home was what I deserved.

That made me think of Mom. She'd be worried that I hadn't checked in like I promised, but probably still didn't know anything was wrong. Tears rolled down my cheeks thinking of what she would do when she found out I was missing. First my dad had left her and now I'd done the same. What would she do? What would *I* do? I opened my eyes and watched Bruno snore for a few minutes.

Who was missing Bruno? Was anyone?

While we'd been walking he'd told me a little about his life in and out of foster homes. Right now he was living with Brother Jackson, or had been. He didn't know his parents, or even remember anything from when he was a child...I mean a smaller child, because I guess he was still a child. Whatever...

Hugging Mom was the last thing that went through my mind as I finally drifted off.

I woke up to someone turning out Bruno's pockets. Of

course the big boy didn't even notice. He was still sound asleep in the same position he'd collapsed in. The only difference was that a river of drool flowed from his open mouth and a snot bubble grew and shrank in time with the rhythm of his snoring.

The figure going through Bruno's stuff was dressed in a long black robe with a hood pulled up to cover his face. He looked like a monk or a druid or something. "Hey!" I shouted as I reached for Lobo's sword.

I wasn't sure why I'd taken the sword instead of burying it with Lobo. It just felt like the thing to do, and the sword was magic. That much was obvious from how Lobo had summoned it from thin air, or how it glowed with a blue aura while he fought with it. But I hadn't been able to figure it out. I tried to make it disappear and re-appear or glow, but it refused to obey my commands.

The druid whipped around and I saw that his face was human. He looked like a young guy, maybe in his late teens or early twenties. His mouth fell open, and he glanced at a pocket knife he'd just stolen from the sleeping Bruno. He quickly hid it behind his back, and began inching toward the exit.

"Go back to sleep, child," he whispered. "This is all a dreeeaaaam." He held up his empty hand and wiggled his fingers as he said the last word, like he was trying to hypnotize me or something.

I jumped up and raised Lobo's sword in an imitation of what I'd seen in fantasy movies. I'm sure I looked stupid, but it was enough to make the druid squeal and leap out of the trailer. That's when I noticed he was wearing roller skates.

He slipped when he landed on the ground, but caught himself and recovered his balance. He glanced back at me and raised Bruno's pocketknife up like it was a prize he'd just won.

"Ha!" he said. "I have your treasure, and with my wheeled boots of swiftness, you won't be able to give chase!" He lurched forward, trying to skate, but repeatedly lost his balance and almost fell.

I didn't follow him, not because I was afraid or because he was too fast, but because I was stunned by his complete inability to skate. He continued to move away, flailing his arms to keep from falling over—which he actually ended up doing once—before he disappeared behind a mound of tires. The whole incident would've seemed weird if it wasn't for… okay, never mind. It was totally weird.

I lowered Lobo's sword and glanced back at Bruno. The big kid was still sleeping. I nudged him with my foot, and he woke with a snort. "I didn't eat your llama, I swear!" he yelled. Then he looked around and smiled sheepishly. "Good morning, Thomas!" He patted the inside of his thighs. "Look, all dry!"

"Come on," I said. "Time to get moving."

He rubbed his eyes, yawned, and then the two of us were off. It was three hours before he realized his pocket knife was missing. I told him about the druid on roller skates, but Bruno still blamed me, and I had to turn out my pockets to convince him I wasn't the thief. Even after that he kept eyeing me suspiciously. I guess "a druid wearing roller skates took your knife" does sound like a pretty lame excuse. Like when I was five and I told Mom that a naked leprechaun riding a camel broke the lamp in the living room. Of course, if we lived in *this* world, that might've been the truth.

My stomach rumbled nonstop, and my mouth was so dry I couldn't suck anymore spit from my tongue. The scout manual of survival said when you were lost without food or water that you should look for certain kinds of berries and a fast moving stream. There were neither here. Just mounds of junk, junk, and more junk.

We did find some blue-glowing mushrooms growing in the shade of an overturned truck, but the ring of dead rats lying around them made me think they might be poisonous. That didn't bother Bruno, and I had to actually step on them and kick the mushrooms to pieces to stop him from eating them. It made him grouchy the rest of the day.

By the time my internal clock was telling me it was night-time again, we had reached the only city on the entire Crossroads planet. Surprisingly, it wasn't made of junk as I'd expected. Instead the whole city was built inside an enormous tower made of black stone that had to be thousands of feet tall. It had no windows, which made it hard to spot against the dark sky, and we'd only caught sight of it because of the comet-like streaks of blue light that continually shot out of the tower. They were quick flashes, like lightning, and never shot out from the same spot twice.

We joined a crowd of others moving steadily through a gigantic, arched doorway. Once inside, I gaped at the thousands of people filling a circular chamber the size of five football fields. They moved up and down a network of staircases that ran around the inner wall of the tower and led to the upper floors. It was chaotic, like that old black and white drawing of stairs going different directions on the walls and ceiling. I think it was drawn by a guy named David Bowie. These staircases had no rails, and occasionally someone would fall off, plummet to the ground, and land in the crowd. Oddly, this didn't seem to bother anyone.

The residents of the tower-city were an odd assortment of creatures. Some were tall and covered in fur—I'm starting to think Bigfoot's actually a refugee from the Crossroads, which I will absolutely write a book about and get rich off of it someday—and some were short and covered in scales. Some looked human, and others looked like crosses between certain animals and people. But the one that shocked me the most was a cyborg penguin-like creature with tank treads for feet. It looked cute—you know in a mutant circus freak sort of way —but let loose a shockingly graphic stream of profanity when Bruno tried to pet it.

It was thanks to that foul-mouthed penguin that I realized everyone was speaking English! Or at least I thought they were. The tower was enchanted to make everyone hear their own language. Guess it was kind of a reverse of the Tower of Babel from the Bible. This made it easier for us to beg for food from a number of shops and restaurants that lined the inner walls. Of course, no one would give us any food, so Bruno and I found a park in the center of the tower's bottom floor and sat on one of the wooden benches, smelling all of the wonderful smells coming from the places that'd rejected us.

We must've looked pretty pathetic, because a big rock creature threw us a couple of crystal coins—that's what they use for money in the tower; transparent glass-like discs etched with the image of a giant tree. He didn't say anything, but just smiled a craggy smile before lumbering on.

I was ecstatic, and asked Bruno to go buy us something that looked and smelled a lot like pizza from one of the furry creatures pushing around a food cart. I was tired, and didn't feel like forcing my way through the crowd again, and it was easier for Bruno because of his size, strength, and total lack of manners. That had been a mistake. I should've gone with him. But instead I lay down on the bench and tried to relax until he came back.

After an hour, I started to get worried. I scanned the crowd looking for him, but it wasn't until I was ready to go look for him that he appeared. He had a big smile on his face, and conspicuously no pizza.

"Where's the food?"

Bruno's smile faded. "What?"

"The food!" I snapped. "That you were supposed to buy!"

"I didn't buy food, I bought this!" Bruno pulled something out of his pocket.

It was a rusty old harmonica.

He raised it to his lips and blew, making a sound that was something like the Auto-Tuned honk of a feral goose.

I lost it.

"Idiot!" I shouted.

Bruno stopped blowing and just stared at me. His lip began to quiver and tears filled his eyes, but it wasn't enough to make my anger fade.

"That was our only money! Now what're we going to do for food?"

He held up a half-eaten sandwich that was green with mold. "I saved you the other half of a sandwich I found in the bathroom..."

I slapped it from his hand.

Bruno was full on crying now. "I thought you were my friend, Thomas!" he shouted. "But you're just like all the other mean kids! You're stupid, you suck, and I hate you!"

He turned and ran away, disappearing into the crowd of freaks before I could call him back, or apologize. I felt sick. Probably not as sick as I would've felt if I'd tried that sandwich, but still

6

ARVEK

It turns out they did keep a day and night schedule inside the tower-city. I sat in the park as the shops closed their doors, and watched the people begin leaving the tower or climbing to the upper levels. I half expected some kind of space-cop to arrest me for loitering, but no one really cared that I didn't leave and neither did I at that point. So, I decided to try to get some sleep, though I expected hunger and despair would make that difficult. But apparently not eating for two days was getting to me, and I passed out.

I woke up and found the massive tower's first floor completely empty. I was groggy, like I'd been woken up too early, but when I rolled onto my side to go back to sleep, I had another one of those weird visions. Just like when I was fighting Ajii, I saw myself from faraway. I was lying on the park bench as three figures stepped out of the shadows.

When the vision ended, I quickly sat up and grabbed Lobo's sword from underneath the bench. I held it up in front of me, facing the direction I had seen the figures come from in my vision. A tall man and two hunched creatures appeared from the darkness.

I raised the sword a little higher and shouted, "Jackpot!"

Nothing happened. So, I decided to run.

I turned, but hadn't taken two steps before one of the hunched creatures landed in front of me. It had to have made a standing jump and flipped in the air above my head in order to land to block my retreat. Apparently it had superhuman strength.

Not good!

The hunched creature was dressed all in black with a cloth mask covering its face, making it look like a medieval executioner. I raised the sword to swing but the creature shot out a clawed hand and grabbed my wrist, twisting to make me drop Lobo's sword. Then it spun me around, and bent my arm behind my back.

The tall figure and the second hunched creature walked toward me. I gritted my teeth and sucked in a sharp breath when the monster holding my arm squeezed my wrist, its long claws digging into my skin and drawing blood.

The tall figure stopped three feet in front of me. Unlike his hunchbacked bodyguards, he looked human, with long black hair and pale skin. He was wearing a long coat of black leather that buttoned across his chest, and glossy black gloves on his hands. He flashed a smile down at me and I winced as I saw his canines had been filed to points making them look like the fangs of a vampire. The scary kind, not the sparkly kind.

The man reached out his gloved hand and gently cupped

my chin. "How did you do it?" He asked in a silky, almost gentle voice.

"Do what?" The arm twisting made me sound like I was going to cry, which I probably was.

"Kill Ajii. He was, after all, a very powerful Dreja. He would've been one of us if he hadn't been so unstable."

My only answer was a sob.

The man glanced at the creature behind me and it let go of my arm. It walked around me, and stood next to its fellow.

"Lobo helped you," the man said as he eyed the sword on the ground.

"Who are you?" I asked, rubbing my wrist and trying to sound brave.

The man grinned, again showing off his creepy vampire teeth. "My name is Arvek." He stepped back and made a dramatic bow.

My voice trembled as I said, "You're a Dreja, aren't you?"

"Yes, I am." Arvek straightened. "But I'm not an insane monster like Ajii."

"Lobo said that all Dreja were monsters and that…"

"Lobo's dead," Arvek cut in. "And you're trapped here with no way home."

"I'll find a bridge back to Earth," I said, proud of myself for sounding a little tough. That was until Arvek laughed at me.

"I'm afraid that your situation is far more desperate than you realize," he said. "Bridge use costs money, of which you have none. I will also wager that you haven't eaten for a while?"

My traitorous stomach picked that very moment to growl.

Arvek grinned. "Even if you were not to starve and somehow earn enough to get someone to open a bridge for you, no magician here knows of your world. It's somewhat disconnected from the rest of the cosmos. That's why it was such a perfect prison for Ajii. You can search the rest of your life and you won't find anyone who can send you home."

"Lobo found a way!"

"Lobo cheated. And believe me when I tell you that duplicating his little stunt is far less likely than your finding a bridge to Earth."

Something told me he was telling the truth.

"Fortunately for you, I am the servant of a being who has the power to open a passage for you back to Earth and can do so without having to find a dimensional soft spot."

When I didn't respond, Arvek said, "Don't believe me? Well, here, I'll prove it."

He extended a hand and drew a two-foot-long, glowing, blue line in the open air before me. A blast of wind exploded outward as the line opened up into a window. I looked through the hole in the air and gasped when I saw Mom riding in a car with Brother Jackson's wife. She was trying to call me on her phone and I could tell she'd been crying a lot because her eyes were red.

"She's driving to the canyon. She knows something's wrong."

Mom started to look around as if she'd heard me. "Thomas?"

"Mom I'm here!" I shouted, but it was too late. Arvek had made the portal vanish by the time I'd gotten the words out. I looked up at the slender man, realization dawning on me. "You want something from me, don't you?"

"Clever boy." Arvek stared at me until I had to look away. Then he said, "Lobo left you with something."

I shook my head. "Lobo didn't give me anything, except for a lightning wand, but I broke it."

"Ah, but he did. I still don't know how he accomplished it, but he passed ownership of something to you—a crystal shard. The master that I serve wants that crystal."

I thought that after what I'd seen in the last few days nothing more could surprise me, but what Arvek was saying totally threw me. "I don't know anything about a crystal shard."

Arvek ignored that and continued talking. "As the owner of this crystal, you have the ability to sense its location the closer to it you get."

"I really don't..."

Arvek raised a hand and I shut up. "I don't know its exact location, but I do know where to look for it." Arvek lowered his hand. "You will go to the thirty-fourth level of this city where you will be met by a guide. He will pay passage for you to a world called Iskarin and will lead you to the general location of Lobo's crystal where you will be able to divine it's hiding place."

"And if I bring it to you, you'll send me home?"

Arvek's smile returned. "And that oaf of a friend of yours, if you wish it."

Suddenly I felt the same cold feeling I'd felt when Ajii was asking me to free him. It was a warning and I knew it. But, just like I'd done before, I ignored it because I was afraid; afraid of Arvek, and afraid of being trapped at the Crossroads forever. I guess I hadn't learned anything.

I stared down at my sneakers. "Ok."

"Then we have a deal!" Arvek clapped his gloved hands together.

The cold pit in my stomach got colder.

Arvek reached into his coat pocket and pulled out a small bag. He shook it, and I heard clacking. He handed me the bag, and said, "You will need supplies. For the journey will take you through unpopulated wilderness." He turned to walk away and his two hunched goons obediently followed; all three disappearing back into the shadows.

"Wait!" I called. "How will I find you once I have the crystal?"

"*I* will find *you*," Arvek's voice echoed from the darkness. Then he was gone.

I opened the bag he'd given me and found five crystal discs—Crossroads money. I looked up, but could only see three floors. The tower was tall, taller even than the Chinese skyscraper I saw two college students climb on YouTube. First thing in the morning I would go find Bruno, and then we'd do as Arvek said. It was my only way home.

7

RAT BREAD

I commenced my search for Bruno in the tower-city's main market. When I didn't find him there, I checked the various eateries, and then moved to the rougher part of the tower-city where most of the bars were located. I tried to avoid eye contact with all the creepy tough-looking aliens staring at me, and for the most part succeeded in avoiding much attention. Except when something very large, like elephant large, stopped me as I walked past where it loitered on the walkway.

I couldn't tell exactly what it was because it was wearing a red cloak with the hood drawn up. But it hissed like a snake and asked if I wanted to buy some psilocybin—said they'd show me wondrous things. I didn't know exactly what *psilocybin* were, but I suspected they weren't magic beans. Well, I guess with magic being real and all they could've been. But if they were magic beans, they were probably less likely to grow a stratospheric beanstalk as they were to land me in rehab.

"No, thanks."

D.A.R.E. Officer Jenkins would be so proud of me. Maybe now he'd return my letters and I'd finally get the pencil and bumper-sticker denied me because my sixth-grade teacher couldn't do an accurate headcount! The nerve of her teaching *us* math! Yeah...I'm still bitter.

I hurried away from the creature and strode toward a place called "The Long Pig Tavern." Sounded like a light-hearted, friendly place.

I pushed through a set of saloon-like double doors and was hit with a blast of foul smelling smoke. It kinda smelled like cigarette smoke, but spicier, like incense. The place was a bizarre combination of the typical outlaw bar you'd see in spaghetti westerns and one of those seasonal Halloween stores. Yeah...*bizarre* was quickly becoming my new *normal*.

I gaped as I took in the wild assortment of intimidating creatures. There was a table full of what I could only describe as "pig-men in pirate costumes" playing cards with piles of crystal coins on the table. They snarled and one tested the point of a dagger as a man in a black cloak put down his cards and collected the pile of transparent discs. I also saw three women that looked like cartoon witches surrounding a bubbling caldron, and my stomach turned when a severed finger surfaced in their stew.

There were also less human-like creatures: a winged eyeball hovering near a staircase in the back, a blue, egg-shaped thing with wiggling tentacles tottering around the room, and clusters of small fur-balls rolling around the floor looking for crumbs and loose change. I guess booze and bad habits had the power to bring even as varied a crowd as this together, because everyone looked like they were having fun, or at least were comfortable.

I walked up to the bar where a very large, very hairy man wearing an apron stood polishing the counter with a filthy rag. I would've took him for human if he hadn't been the size of a small bus. He had an eyepatch, was missing teeth, and a part of his left ear looked to have been burned off. It was the kind of face only a mother could love, and only if that mother was drunk and half blind.

He wiped his nose with a tattooed forearm, and snorted loudly as he worked circles on the bar with his nearly black rag. "What can I get for you, stranger?" he asked in a gruff voice.

He didn't actually look up at me until I started talking. "Have you seen a big kid with blond hair, wearing clothes like mine?"

He squinted at me with his one good eye. "You a soldier?"

"A soldier?" I scoffed. "Why would you..." He was staring at my scout uniform. *Huh,* I thought. *Maybe C.J. had been onto something.*

"I'm not a soldier. I'm just looking for my friend."

"Yeah, I seen him," he finally said. Then he went back to scrubbing the counter, although now his dirty rag was leaving smudges of black.

I waited a minute, and when it became obvious the barkeep wasn't going to say anymore, I asked, "Well, can you tell me where he is?"

"You gonna buy something?" The big man snapped.

"Y-yeah," I stammered. "Can I get some food?"

The barkeep snorted, this time a particularly long and wet sound, and then spat a wad of phlegm into his cleaning rag. Then he went back to wiping down the bar. I had to look away, and cover my mouth, sure I was going to puke.

"We got bread or meat," the barkeep said.

The topic of food made my stomach growl again, despite my disgust, and I decided that I really did want something to eat. I picked what I thought would be the safer of the two options. "Bread, please."

The barkeep extended an open palm. I quickly dug into the pouch of money Arvek had given me, and produced a large transparent disc the size of a silver dollar. I dropped it in the big hairy guy's hand, not wanting to touch him at all if I could help it. He grinned at the coin, but didn't say whether it was the right amount. Though, now that I think about it, I'm sure that's because I overpaid—jerk.

He reached under the counter, lifted out a squealing rat by its tail, and casually tossed it to the side. Then he pulled out a plate with something black on it and dropped it in front of me.

"Bread," he proclaimed.

I touched it and found it hard like rock. I didn't even try to bite it, afraid that I might break a tooth or cut my cheek. "You said you saw my friend?" I asked.

"Bruno!" the barkeep bellowed, giving me a direct whiff of his disgusting breath.

A moment later Bruno pushed out of the doors to the kitchen. Wearing a dirty apron over his scout uniform, he was dangling a squealing rat by its tail with one hand, and gripping the handle of a large knife in the other.

"This guy wants to talk to you!" The barkeep motioned at me before turning and clomping away.

"Hi, Bruno," I said not able to meet his eyes.

"Hello, Thomas," Bruno replied coolly. "If that is your real name."

I wasn't sure how to respond to that. Clearly Bruno was still upset.

"You're looking well," he said in that same cold tone. The rat squealed, folded up on itself and bit at Bruno's knuckles, but the big guy didn't seem to notice.

"Look, Bruno. I'm sorry I yelled at you and called you an idiot. I didn't mean it." I extended my hand. "Friends?"

Bruno stared at my hand and then a wide grin spread across his face. He dropped both the rat and the knife and wrapped his meaty arms around me and lifted me off the floor.

"I can't breathe!" I wheezed.

Bruno let go and I dropped to the ground. "Sorry," he said with a giggle.

I shook my head and smiled. "We're good."

"Hey!" The big barkeep shouted at us. "None of that out here. The hugging room is in the back!"

I didn't really know what the barkeep was talking about, and I didn't really want to know. I showed Bruno the bag of crystal coins Arvek had given me. "Wanna go get something to eat?"

Bruno glanced at the bar where my plate of untouched petrified bread sat. "You didn't like my rat bread?"

I took another look at the black bread, noticing for the first time the tail sticking out of the end of the loaf. It made me *very* glad I hadn't tried to eat it. I shrugged apologetically.

"Hey, it's better than these so called chips!" Bruno grabbed a hand full of poker chips from his pocket and popped one in his mouth. He winced when he bit down and then grimaced as he forced a swallow. "I think they're stale!"

"And yet, you're still eating them," I said.

"Well yeah, but..."

"Look, Bruno, I found a way home," I interrupted.

"Really?!" Bruno shouted and made to hug me again, but I held up a hand.

"No hugging, remember?"

Bruno glanced at the barkeep who gave us a sharp nod.

"I met someone who knows the way back home. His name is Arvek and he'll send us home if we do a job for him."

"Yay!" Bruno shouted and clapped.

I *shushed* him with a finger to my lips, and then glanced around to make sure we hadn't attracted anyone's attention. The pig-men were giving us dirty looks, and their friend in the cloak was hiding his face behind a fan of playing cards.

"What job do we gotta do?" Bruno asked. "Something fun?!"

I looked away from the card players and lowered my voice, hoping Bruno would get the hint and stay quiet. "We have to find a crystal for him. It's not on this planet though, so we have to go up to the thirty-fourth level and find a portal to a world called Iskarin. Arvek said he'd send a guide to help us. After we get the crystal, he'll send us home."

Bruno smiled. "Really?"

"Really."

Bruno smothered me with another bear hug, and I swear this time I could feel my ribs start to crack.

"Hey!" The barkeep snapped. "What did I say?" This time he pointed to a door behind the counter with a sign hanging above it.

The sign read *Hugging Room.*

Bruno abruptly let me go, and I nearly fell when I landed back on my feet. I looked at the barkeep who was growling at us.

"I think we should get out of here," I whispered to Bruno.

He nodded and took off his apron. We turned and began to make our way to the exit.

"Bruno!" the barkeep shouted. "Where do you think you're going? Those squid eyes aren't going to pickle themselves!"

"Iskar..." Bruno began.

I cut him off. "Lunch break!"

"You know the rule; five-minute break for every forty-eight-hour shift. Clock's ticking, boy!" The barkeep went back to "cleaning" the counter. Come to think of it, I don't think I saw him pour a single drink. I think all he did was polish the counter with his filthy rag. I later asked Bruno about it, but all he did was laugh, and say "Yeah."

Just then a centaur emerged from the Hugging Room holding the shiny metal hand of what could best be described as a robot clown.

It was time to go.

We left the tavern together, Bruno too excited to complain much about losing a job he later described as having "great opportunities for advancement in an exciting career field." I think he watched too many commercials back home.

From that day things were different between us. I think it's because that was the day we really became friends.

8

THE GUIDE

After buying bags, food, and water, we started the long climb up to the thirty-fourth floor. Bruno didn't like the fact that we had to climb the tower stairs, and I can't say that I blamed him. We had to have climbed over five hundred steps, and by the end we were stopping to rest for five minutes on every floor.

The tower's upper levels were very different from the ground level. While that had been full of shops and buildings, the upper levels were just circular floors with arched doorways spaced every twenty feet or so along the inner wall of the tower. Each of those doorways was a portal to another world, and crowds of people stood in line to travel through them. It kind of reminded me of the airport.

The thirty-fourth floor was not as crowded as the levels below, but people still milled about, coming and going through the different archways. Red-robed mages wearing masks stood in front of the doorways, and collected money before casting spells and ushering people through portals. It took some asking before we found an attendant—an orangutan wearing a top hat, monocle, and something that looked suspiciously like a diaper—who could show us the doorway to Iskarin. It was unmanned, so the red-furred ape tottered off to get one of the masked mages to open it for us.

"Our guide must be late," I said while glancing around. Arvek hadn't told me who or what our guide would be, only that they'd meet us here.

"So you have finally come!" a voice from behind made me jump.

I spun around to find a familiar face looking down at me from under a drawn hood. It was the black-robed druid, the one who'd robbed us the day before.

"You!" I took a step toward him.

"Him!" Bruno said in a tone that mimicked mine. Then he glanced at me. "Thomas who is that guy?"

"*I* am *your* guide," the man said.

"No, you're the guy who stole Bruno's pocket knife!"

"So you weren't making that up?" Bruno said, cocking his head.

The druid's eyes widened. "Uh...yes. That was...a test...to see how you handled..."

"You said he wore roller skates," Bruno said in an accusatory tone, as if he still didn't believe me.

"Alas," the druid said with a theatrical sigh. "I lost my boots of swiftness in a game of chance."

"And you're an interdimensional guide?"

"You do not recognize the robes of a sage from the floating fortress of Tildar?!"

"Whoa," Bruno said sounding impressed, even though I

knew he had no idea what the floating fortress of Tildar was.

"What does that have to do with it?"

The druid straightened. "It is beyond your meager powers of comprehension. Suffice it to say, I have been guiding brave travelers, such as yourselves, across the cosmos for over four-hundred years."

"You look twenty."

"Ah," the druid said holding up one finger. "Infinite are the mysteries of the infinite cosmos."

Bruno giggled. "He said infinite twice."

A commotion near the stairs caught my attention. Our monocle sporting orangutan friend was being accosted by the group of pirate pig-men I'd seen playing cards in the tavern.

The druid nervously glanced at the group of pig-men.

"It was *you* in the tavern playing cards with those pig pirates!"

"Shhh! Not so loud!" The druid pled. "Now it is time for us to commence your noble quest." He began pushing me toward the Iskarin archway.

"I don't have any money left to pay for a mage to open a portal. Did Arvek give you enough money to buy us passage?"

"Yes-yes," the druid replied as he broke into a swift stride. "Aardvark gave me plenty of coin. Now do not dawdle. The Gorithanu of Hilmtar are vargassing the plain."

"Oh no!" Bruno said. "Not them!" Again, I knew he had no clue what the druid was talking about. Come to think of it, neither did I.

I looked back toward the stairs and found one of the pig-men pointing a dagger at us. The rest of his group looked our way, then shoved the diapered ape aside and began to push through a crowd of people toward us.

"Run!" the druid shouted and we all broke for the Iskarin gate.

We reached the gate just as one of the masked mages took his place behind a stone plinth. He extended his hand and announced in a bored tone, "Ten crystal drachma per traveler."

I looked at the druid, but he wouldn't meet my eyes. "Hey!" I hissed.

The druid looked at me in mock-surprise, as though he had just been shaken from sleep. "Oh, of course." He chuckled nervously as he drew a brown bag from within his robes.

He handed the mage the entire bag. "Keep the change."

The masked mage took the bag and chanted something. A hole appeared in the air, just like when Ajii had torn space back in Caesar's Palace. The portal opened up to a world with a blue sky and tree covered green hills stretching into the distance.

"Hey!" the masked mage shouted. He lifted up his mask and glowered at us. "This is just a bag of bottle caps!" At the same time the leader of the group of pig-men, distinguishable by his jewel encrusted eyepatch and a skeletal parrot sloppily tied to his shoulder, started snorting and squealing at us.

"Go!" The druid yelled and then shoved me through the hole in the air.

I scraped my palms on loose rocks and slid to a stop face down in grass and weeds. I had just risen to my knees when Bruno landed on top of me.

"Bruno!" I yelled in a muffled voice.

Bruno rolled off my back, and sheepishly said, "Sorry."

The druid stood a few feet away and dusted himself off. "Follow me!" he ordered.

We broke into a run away from a stone archway identical to the one back in the tower-city. It looked out of place just free-standing in the grass connected to nothing, like it was all that remained of an ancient ruined castle or something.

We ran toward a thicket of bushes and crawled underneath them. There we waited for almost an hour, watching the archway to see if anyone followed us, but no one came through.

"Why were those pig guys chasing you?" I finally asked.

"They are soldiers of the Ninth Terror, agents of chaos and darkness. They are after my soul and the power it would give them."

"And it had absolutely nothing to do with the fact that you just cheated them at cards?" I said in a flat tone.

"Eh." The druid shrugged. "Nobody likes losing money, not even demon beasts from the hills of Grimdar."

"Is that the only gate back?" I pointed at the stone archway.

"Of course not, young..." the druid hesitated.

"Thomas. My name is Thomas! Didn't Arvek tell you that?"

"Of course he did!" The druid chuckled nervously. "Now let's stop wasting time with silly questions!" He climbed out from underneath the bushes and pointed at a road leading off into the distance. "Onward!"

9

THE BRIDGE MONSTER

We trudged along through tall grass as the druid led us off the road and up the side of a hill. I tried to ask him questions, but each time he would respond with crazy ramblings. He reminded me of a hobo that used to live under a viaduct near the soup kitchen back home. I think the guy's name was Reggie? Anyway, I once caught him having a heated argument with a half inflated beach ball; half inflated because he was stabbing it with a shiv wrapped in duct tape.

When we finally reached the top of the hill, a wide chasm came into view. It ran north and south as far as I could see without any narrow spots to jump across.

"How we gonna get to the other side?" I asked.

The druid just stared at me with a stupid look on his face. "Um...how do *you* think we should get to the other side?"

Bruno laughed. "Thomas, that reminds me of a joke. Wanna hear it?"

I ignored Bruno and stepped closer to the druid. "Aren't *you* the guide?"

"Of course I am!" He pointed further down the path. "We shall go this way!"

"Hey, what's that?" Bruno asked.

I turned to find Bruno pointing opposite the direction the druid had pointed. I shaded my eyes and squinted. It looked like a house sitting on top of the chasm.

"I think that's a covered bridge!" I shouted, and then broke into a jog toward it.

"Yay for Bruno!" Bruno clapped and followed me.

The druid caught up to me and I glared at him. "How come you didn't know about the bridge?"

The druid shrugged. "It's been a while since I've come this way."

"How long?" I asked.

"Years!" the druid blurted out quickly. "Many, many, many, many years...many years."

I was starting to think the druid was an impostor, but I wasn't sure. Everything I'd experienced since leaving Earth was so weird that I really couldn't know for sure. So, I let him continue to "lead" us.

We jogged for close to an hour, having to slow our pace when Bruno started to lag behind. Eventually we were forced to stop and wait for him at the bottom of a hill just beneath the entrance to the covered bridge. I pulled out some water bottles we'd bought before leaving The Crossroads and took a long drink. The druid seated himself on a fallen log, and we rested until Bruno stumbled over to us. He was so winded that he couldn't even speak. I tossed him the water bottle and watched him drink it dry.

When he was done, he dropped the bottle and pointed over my shoulder. "Hey, what's that?"

He shoved past me to a tangle of brush and began clearing away the weeds, revealing a wooden sign. It was made of old, splintering wood and had a sloppy painting of something that looked like a green ghost wearing sunglasses and a hat. Words were written on the sign, but they were barely legible, like a pre-school kid had written them in crayon.

BEWARE OF THE BRIDGE MONSTER!

Bruno started to sound out the words. "Be... be...be waree...be waree of the...of the..."

"Beware of the bridge monster," I finished for him.

"Bridge monster?" Bruno squealed and grabbed my arm really tight.

"Ow!" I said as I pulled my arm free. "Don't be a girl! There's no monster here!"

"Don't be so sure," the druid said in a warning tone.

"What are you talking about?"

The druid stood, and intoned, "The monks of Alaten say that a horrible monster guards this bridge."

"You didn't even know this bridge was here!" I snapped.

"Maybe not. But I knew the monster was here," the druid said.

"There's no bridge monster!" I shouted, and then started climbing up the hill, determined to prove it.

When I got to the top I found a dirt road leading into the open doorway of a building that looked like an old barn.

"Thomas!" Bruno shrieked.

I turned to look down the hill at him and the druid, who

was now standing a little behind Bruno like he was afraid. They looked like they had just started to climb up after me before stopping.

"What's your problem, Bruno?" I said. "You fought Ajii! How could you be scared of an imaginary—" I looked back at the entrance to the bridge and froze, "—monster."

Peeking out from just inside the covered bridge's doorway was a person wearing sunglasses and a black, wide brimmed hat. Though, I realized immediately that I wasn't looking at a person. People didn't have wet looking green skin, and they usually had arms. This creature didn't have arms. He reminded me of a cartoonish Halloween ghost. You know, the kind that's pretty much just a white sheet draped over some poor kid whose single mother didn't have the money for an Iron Man costume and the other kids stole his candy and made him sing Disney theme songs to get it back. Yeah, I'm talking about me.

The green ghost looking thing with sunglasses and a black hat glided—I say glided because it didn't have feet or legs—out of the dark and onto the road toward me. It stopped just in front of the entrance. Now that I could see it in the light, it looked like it was made of green Jello; if that Jello were alive and trying to look like a spy from an old comic strip.

I caught myself staring. "Hi." I waved.

The thing didn't do or say anything.

I took a step toward it. "So's this your bridge?"

This time the creature made a noise, but it wasn't in any language I could understand. In fact, I wasn't even sure it was talking because I saw no mouth. It wasn't telepathic, not like

Ajii because I heard real sound *outside* my head. It mumbled, its tone rising and falling sharply. It sounded mad. The enchantment of the tower-city to allow everyone to understand each other was a permanent thing that stayed with anyone who traveled from The Crossroads, so if this was a real language, I should've been able to understand it.

I went on anyway, hoping that it could understand *me*. "See, the thing is, my friends and I need to use your bridge. That cool?"

I took another step forward, and the creature started to talk louder in its gibberish language. I glanced back at the druid. "Do you know what it wants?"

"It demands that you best it in hand to hand combat if you wish to cross its bridge."

"It doesn't have hands," Bruno said.

I turned back to look at the creature, and laughed. "Listen, slimy green...dude. I don't want to hurt you. So why don't you just let us pass, ok?" I tried to walk past, but it molded a tentacle from its body and knocked me back. For being made of Jello it was surprisingly strong. I felt my chest where it'd struck me. My shirt wasn't wet with slime as I'd expected, but my skin did sting from the slap.

"You hit me!"

I moved around the bridge monster, this time walking in a wide arc so I was a dozen feet away. Before I could pass, it shot out another green tentacle and tripped me. I fell flat onto the wooden boards that made up the bridge, scraping my hands and getting at least three slivers.

"That's it!" I leapt to my feet and threw a punch at the creature.

Now, I never had been a fighter—I was always too skinny —but I've seen a lot of ninja movies, and practiced staff twirling in the back yard. It didn't help. The moment I landed a punch, the green dude turned its skin hard like rock. I yelped as my knuckles popped, and then pulled my hand back and cradled it against my chest. It hurt, but I didn't think I'd broken anything, probably because I punched like a girl. A weak girl, not like Susie Sorenson, my six-year-old neighbor. She broke my nose after I took her turn on our backyard trampoline.

I looked up at the bridge monster just in time to take a tentacle slap to the face. It hit me so hard that I actually spun backward and fell again, this time on the dirt road that led up to the bridge. After that I wasn't even able to stand. Every time I tried I got whacked with another of the bridge monster's tentacles. The beating continued even when I stayed down.

Crack! A tendril whipped me in the back of my head.

Thunk! A tendril with a hard, blocky end crashed down on my back.

Whap! A tendril forming a paddle slapped my butt.

I didn't think the blows were hard enough to cause any real damage, but they sure did hurt—like when someone tags you with a rolled up towel—and they made it impossible for me to get away. I was covering my face, trying not to get a bloody nose, when I heard Bruno stomp onto the bridge.

The bridge monster gibbered out a loud challenge to which Bruno screamed "That's my friend!"

I uncovered my eyes just in time to see Bruno backhand the bridge monster. It cried out in its gibbering language and retreated a few paces. I climbed to my feet and stood next to Bruno who had his arms folded. For a second he actually looked like a tough guy.

"Do you yield?" I shouted at the bridge monster.

It replied with a stream of angry gibberish.

"Do-you-yield?!"

As if I'd ordered him, Bruno took a step toward the bridge monster and summoned his silver club.

Apparently the bridge monster did yield, because it slid aside and allowed me to pass. Bruno and the druid followed, and we walked onto the covered bridge. When we came out the other side, I looked back and saw that the creature was following us.

"Hey!" I yelled.

Bruno turned around and raised his silver club.

The creature stopped and muttered something that sounded sad, like it was sorry, and wanted to be friends.

I glanced at the druid and asked, "What's it saying?"

The druid listened for a moment. "He says that because you defeated him, he is sworn to serve you."

"*He* wants to come with us?"

"He says that it is the way of his people."

"No!" I waved my arm through the air. "Go back to guarding your stupid bridge!"

Seeming to have gotten the message, the bridge monster stayed still and made a sad sounding mumble. I turned and started walking away.

"Ah, he looks sad," Bruno said. "Let's give him a hug!"

"I'm not worried about his feelings, Bruno." I turned to our "guide." "Where to now, Druid?"

"Um," the druid said as he stupidly surveyed a fork in the dirt road ahead. "I shall consult the spirits!" He sat down on the ground cross-legged, holding his arms out as if to meditate.

"What are you...?"

"Silence!" he barked. "You must also close your eyes and listen to the music of the fates!"

Bruno obediently clenched his eyes shut.

"Fine," I said with a sigh and then closed my eyes. After a few quiet moments I thought I heard what sounded like a coin being tossed in the air. I opened my eyes just in time to see the druid stuff something back into his robe.

"The spirits have spoken to me!" He stood and pointed to the left path of the fork. "We shall go that way!" He confidently strode forward.

"Come on, Bruno," I said as I massaged my aching knuckles.

Bruno tripped and fell to the ground, nearly knocking me over in the process.

"You can open your eyes now, Bruno."

10

ZOMBIEVILLE

"Shoo!" I shouted and waved my arm in the air, but it didn't do any good. The bridge monster just kept following us as soon as I turned my back.

"Why is he following us?" I growled.

"Maybe he's lonely," Bruno said.

I turned around again, and again the creature stopped and stared at me from behind those stupid sunglasses. This time I screamed, "Go away!" But when I turned back I could hear its soft, gibbering mumbles growing louder and knew it hadn't listened.

"He likes us!" Bruno said. "Can we keep him?"

"He's not a puppy, Bruno!" I snapped. "He's a…" I hesitated. What was the bridge monster anyway? "Druid, you seemed to know what it wanted back there. Do you know what it is?"

"He is part of an ancient race of beings known as the Sokal Tarium Vesta Tharr!"

"Did you just make that up?" I asked.

"Of course not!" The druid protested. "He *is* one of the Halsik Gorem Septa Obon."

"Wait, that's not the name you said the first..."

"...In fact, he is the lost king of his people!"

"Right." I was now almost sure the druid was a fraud, and was hoping that if he was, Arvek's real guide would find us. "Well can you tell him to stop following us?"

"*I* don't speak his language," the druid said.

I finally lost my temper. "AHHHH!" I picked up a rock, turned and hurled it at the bridge monster.

It fell short by three feet. I wasn't very athletic, all right? And the rock was really heavy! Don't judge me!

The creature cocked its head to the side and softly mumbled something.

I turned away again and sucked in a deep breath to calm myself. "Fine. Let him follow. But everyone ignore him and pretend he isn't here. Maybe then he'll lose interest and go away."

"That's what people usually do with me!" Bruno proudly exclaimed.

I tried that for an hour, and so did the druid. Bruno, on the other hand, kept turning back to smile and wave. At one point he even asked if we had any breadcrumbs so he could feed the bridge monster like the ducks at the park. After that I gave up trying to run him off and he fell in with us.

We walked for a long time. Eventually the grass and trees became less frequent and we found ourselves traveling over a barren plain of hard, flat rock. I was thirsty hungry and tired, and something inside me told me we were going the wrong way. My worry got so strong that I couldn't stand it any longer. I walked up to the druid and grabbed his arm.

He stopped and turned to look at me. "What is it?"

"Where are we going?"

The druid opened his mouth and raised his eyebrows, trying to look like he was hurt, but I knew it was fake. "Why we're going to," he hesitated, "your destination of course..."

I folded my arms. "We're lost, aren't we?"

"Never! I know exactly where we are and where we're headed."

"Really? Ok, so lay it out for me."

The druid glanced around desperately before finally pointing at a dilapidated sign hanging on a wooden pole a short distance ahead. "There's a town not far from here; a place for us to rest and resupply." The druid broke into a sprint, jogging toward the sign.

I followed, but stopped when I caught sight of what was written on the sign.

ZOMBIEVILLE – 5 MILES

"Are you serious?" I yelled. "Zombieville?"

The druid dismissively waved a hand. "It's just the name of the town. One of those deliberately ironic names intended to be a joke. I assure you that Zombieville is as safe as a baby's crib."

"A baby's crib?!" Bruno shrieked.

I ignored that and asked, "You've been there?"

"Oh yes, many times," the druid answered. "In spite of its name, Zombieville is a lively town where all our needs can be met. It's a quaint hamlet, its cobblestone streets filled with all kinds of festivities and culture!"

Zombieville,

was a ghost town.

The place looked like something out of a horror movie with its old windmill that rattled as it slowly turned, and the cawing of a crow that watched us from the roof of one of the abandoned buildings. A tumbleweed even bounced along in front of us right as we were passing the town's welcome sign. Zombieville itself was made up of clusters of old houses that no health inspector would hesitate to condemn. A dirt street stretched down the center of town lined by an old-west style boardwalk that ran along a row of boarded up shops.

"Lively town, huh?" I said to the druid.

He chuckled nervously. "I must've been thinking of a *different* Zombieville."

"Right," I said with an eye roll. "Well, we're here, and it'll be getting dark soon. We might as well camp for the night." I opened my water bottle and tried to squeeze the last few drops onto my tongue.

"I'm hungry," Bruno whined.

I shook my water bottle, then capped it and put it back in my bag. "Maybe we should split up and go look for a well, or something to eat."

"An excellent idea!" The druid said. "Come Thomas. I shall accompany you, and..."

"I'm going with Bruno. You can go with," I stared at the bridge monster before saying, "the green dude."

The bridge monster gibbered what sounded like an offended reply, and I got the impression he was saying "that's not my name," but I didn't care. The sensitivities of a gelatinous ghost traveling incognito were the least of my worries at the moment.

"Let's meet back here in an hour, ok?"

We broke apart and headed for different ends of the boardwalk. I ran a hand through my hair and sighed. I wasn't sure what to do. Clearly the druid was an imposter who'd just used us to escape the pig pirates that were trying to kill him. I thought about just sneaking off with Bruno and leaving the druid and the green dude behind, but I dismissed the thought. Not because I'd feel guilty, but because I just didn't know where to go. I decided to ask Bruno what he thought.

"I think the druid isn't Arvek's guide," I said.

Bruno stopped walking and stared at me with his mouth hanging open. "But he's a sage of the floating fortress of Tildar."

"You don't even know what that is!"

"Sure I do," he said not meeting my eyes.

I groaned. "That conman is rubbing off on you."

"Eew." Bruno wiped at his clothes.

I just shook my head and walked toward a building that looked like it could be a store. The door was all boarded up, but Bruno easily smashed through it with his silver club. The sun was starting to set, making it dark inside the abandoned shop. It took my eyes a minute to adjust, but when they did, I saw a row of shelves tipped over onto one another like fallen dominos. There were jars all over the wooden floor, most broken, but some still full of preserved fruit or pickled vegetables. I caught Bruno trying to open a jar of what probably used to be peaches or something like them.

"Don't eat that!" I snapped. "That fruit is probably a hundred years old."

Bruno looked up at me, and scrunched his nose. "But they say it gets better with age."

"That's wine." I snatched the jar away from Bruno.

"But I'm hungry!"

"Then maybe you shouldn't have eaten through all of your supplies an hour after we got..."

A vision flashed in my head. Like before, it was as if I were watching myself from outside my body. I saw Bruno and I standing in the store staring at a boarded up window as a pair of arms broke through. They were followed by more arms, and then people.

A sound snapped me out of my trance. It was moaning, like someone was in pain; quiet at first but quickly getting louder. Then more moaning came from outside in a different direction.

Glass broke.

I jumped, and Bruno screamed when two white arms pushed through one of the boarded up windows. It was just like what I'd seen a moment before in my mind.

Another pair of arms broke through the remaining planks of wood, and I caught a glimpse of what was trying to get in. There were half a dozen humans, or at least they had started out human. They looked really pale, and their faces were covered in large gashes, and one even had a gaping hole where his eye should've been. Their teeth were black, and their clothes were tattered and torn.

"Zombies!" I shouted.

Bruno hid behind me, whimpering like a scared dog.

"YOUR CLUB!"

Bruno summoned his silver club and pointed it at the zombies. They had completely broken into the shop and were stumbling over one another as they climbed in through the window. I looked to the open door. Only the tiniest bit of light remained in the sky, and I couldn't even see the sun. I was about to bolt out the shop's front door, but it was crowded by more zombies. I drew Lobo's sword, holding it awkwardly in front of me.

"What do we do, Thomas?" Bruno sounded on the edge of tears.

I glanced around the shop and my attention focused on an old staircase. I made a break for it, barely evading a zombie as it reached for me. Bruno had to baseball-swing his club into its face before he could follow. The zombie's moaning cut off as it crumpled to the floor. I raced up the stairs, but one of the wooden steps collapsed under my weight, my foot plunging through and getting stuck. I managed to yank my leg free, the broken wood raking my ankle as I scrambled up to the next step.

Bruno took the steps two at a time, missing all the rotted boards and actually passing me on the way up. We reached the second floor which looked like an apartment with old couches, tables, and a bed in the corner. There were holes in the floor where the wood had rotted away, and I could see down into the store below. Dozens of zombies swarmed over the fallen shelves, shoving over one another in an attempt to reach the staircase.

One clambered up the stairs and Bruno knocked it back down into a rolling heap with his silver club. "Where do we go now?" He struck another zombie trying to crawl up the stairs.

I desperately scanned the room, hoping for another staircase to the roof, but it looked like this was it. There was a large open window in the apartment's east wall. I ran to it and looked out. Dark shapes wandered all about the town, but they weren't grouping together like they were downstairs. If we were quick, we could probably avoid them and make it out of Zombieville alive. That was if we could get out of *this store* alive.

The window opened over a slanted roof ending in a drop that couldn't have been more than fifteen feet from the ground. I glanced back at Bruno and shouted, "Come on!"

He kicked a zombie in the chest, causing it to fall back into a group of six. They tumbled down the stairs together and landed in a heap, but already more were climbing over them. Bruno ran over to me and I climbed out onto the roof. He didn't look like he wanted to go, but after glancing back at a zombie who'd just reached the top of the stairs, he eagerly followed me. We sidled along the face of the building until I found a spot on the ground free of zombie traffic.

"We have to jump down," I said.

Bruno's eyes widened. "Can't we just stay here?"

Ignoring that I continued, "We can slide off the roof and land on the boardwalk below. It's not a far drop, so we should be ok."

Bruno just started to whimper.

I was getting frustrated, but I knew yelling at Bruno wouldn't help. So I drew in a deep breath and said, "It's like a slide!"

Bruno stopped whimpering and leaned to look down over the eaves. That's when I pushed him.

He shrieked as he rolled off the roof. I didn't wait for him to land before I followed, sliding down the slope and off the edge. I let go of Lobo's sword as I fell, praying that it didn't hit Bruno, or cut me. I landed on my feet, but lost my balance and fell to the planks of the boardwalk. Bruno was already standing, rubbing his side and glaring at me. He'd actually left an impact crater in the wooden walkway.

"That wasn't nice, Thomas!"

Several wandering zombies took notice of us, and began to shamble over. "Your club!" I hissed.

Bruno summoned his silver club and I found Lobo's sword. It was driven point first into the wood, and I had to work to yank it free. Though, I wasn't really sure what I was going to do with it. For some reason the power it gave Lobo when he fought Ajii wouldn't work for me.

We ran down the boardwalk, back toward the place where we'd entered the town. Two figures burst from a side alley. I raised my sword, but lowered it when I saw who it was. The druid was panting heavily, and the green dude was gibbering fast in a high pitched tone.

"Thomas!" the druid shouted. Then he bent forward and said in between sucking breaths, "Zombieville's...not...safe!"

I was so angry that I wanted to stab the druid with Lobo's sword. The green dude's mumbling gibberish also took on an angry tone as he turned to face the druid.

The druid straightened. "Hey! How was I supposed to know this place was infested with zombies?"

"It's called ZOMBIEVILLE, you idiot!" I snapped.

Bruno tugged on the back of my shirt. He was whimpering and pointing at a group of zombies gathering in front of us. I spun to run in the opposite direction but stopped at the sight of more zombies blocking our way. I glanced around for an escape route but zombies moaned and shuffled coming at us from every direction.

We were surrounded.

A light suddenly streaked into the sky above us, like someone had shot a flare gun. But instead of burning out, the light exploded into a bright orb that hung over the town making it as bright as day. The zombies' moaning changed from low and slow to shrieks of pain. They stopped moving toward us, and began to retreat.

"Follow me!" a voice called from a dozen feet away; a voice that, oddly, sounded familiar. It belonged to a tall man dressed in a brown cloak with the hood drawn up and a scarf wrapping his nose and mouth so that all I could see were his eyes.

"Did you hear me?!" he shouted. "We have to get out of here before my spell burns out!"

I shared a glance with Bruno and then we broke into a run toward the stranger. The druid and the green dude followed us, and before I knew it, we were sprinting past the town's welcome sign and into the darkness.

11

THE CRYSTALS OF DESTINY

I don't know how long we ran, but I had a stitch in my side and my legs were burning by the time mystery man let us stop. As bad of shape as I was in, Bruno was far worse. He stumbled to his knees and then puked. Even the druid was winded and, for once, kept his mouth shut. The green dude had just glided alongside me, and didn't look at all like the sprint away from Zombieville bothered him. Of course, I'm not sure I'd be able to tell if it did. The creature didn't sweat, or breathe or really do anything other than make noises and move. Kinda like a baby; a big, Jello baby with stupid sunglasses and a hat. Ok, so maybe he wasn't anything like a baby.

I plopped down on a fallen log, not caring that my hard landing on the wood grain hurt my tailbone. "Who are you?" I asked once I caught my breath.

"The man who saved your life," he said. Then he turned around.

He took down his hood and removed his face scarf to

reveal that he was human with long black hair, a beardless jaw, and dark eyes. He was young, probably sixteen or seventeen, with an athletic build and the kind of stern face that warned he'd long ago lost his sense of humor.

"My name is Darius," he said.

"Are you Arvek's guide?"

The druid was too winded to say anything, but he did make a noise letting me know he was offended.

Darius nodded. "But I don't work for Arvek. I'm a guardian and Lobo's apprentice."

I suddenly felt shaky inside. "Then I'm sorry to have to be the one to tell you this, but your..."

"I know what happened to him!" Darius snapped. "News like that spreads fast, even across the cosmos."

That made me wonder how everyone knew. Lobo said Earth was isolated from other worlds, but Arvek and Darius acted like it'd been all over the news. *I wonder if there's some kind of cosmic news channel?*

"Then I guess this is yours." I stood and started to draw Lobo's sword, but jumped when it flashed blue and disappeared, only to reappear in Darius's outstretched hand.

"H-how did you do that?" I sputtered. "It wouldn't work for me!"

Darius smirked. "It's a hero blade. It reads the heart of the one who wields it, and will only serve a true hero."

"Oh." I sat back down on the log, Darius's explanation for why I couldn't make the sword work stinging me. I mean, I knew I wasn't a hero, but I thought at least I was brave. I'd killed Ajii hadn't I?

"Do you want to tell me what you were doing in Zombieville after dark?" Darius demanded.

I turned to look at the druid and saw that both Bruno and the green dude were doing the same.

"What?!" The druid said. "How was I supposed to know that we'd crossed into undead territory?"

"So where did you think you were going then?" Darius pointed Lobo's sword at the druid.

The druid raised his chin. "I was leading young Thomas to..." he hesitated, "to...to his destiny!"

"An eternity of undeath?!"

The druid mouth's hung open. "Of course not! I was leading him..."

Darius cut him off. "In the wrong direction!"

Even though I enjoyed watching someone call the druid out on his lies, I really needed the answers Lobo had promised me, so I spoke up. "What do you want with me?"

Darius lowered Lobo's sword and turned to look at me. "I went to great lengths and risked much so as to be the one that Arvek hired as your guide, and I am not going to let all that work go to waste."

"Why do you care what Arvek wants me to do?"

"Because if I don't intervene, you'll be handing him a very powerful treasure; something my father spent his whole life fighting to keep out of the enemy's hands."

Father? I took a hard look at Darius's face, and was surprised I hadn't already noticed the resemblance. Darius had the same square chin and intense stare. It now made sense why his voice had sounded familiar.

"What enemy?"

Darius stared at me for a long time before saying, "My father didn't tell you?"

"No!" I shouted, a tear running down my cheek. "He didn't tell me anything! He just took me away from home and left me alone at The Crossroads with no way to survive!" I stood up. "And now you're taking away the last hope I have by telling me I can't give this crystal to the one person who has the power to send me home!"

Darius's angry frown faded and he inhaled. Then he slipped Lobo's sword beneath his leather belt so it hung at his hip. I wiped my eyes and sniffed, trying not to look at Bruno or the others.

"I am sorry, I truly am. I'm sure my father didn't intend for you to get stranded or mixed up in all of this." Darius ran a hand over his face. "But you need to understand that there is something much bigger going on here than the plight of one lost boy."

I sat back down on the log and bowed my head. "Like what?"

"Arvek is one of the knights of Adrayen. Have you heard that name yet?"

I shook my head.

"I have," the druid said raising his hand. "Portly fellow with an overbite, red hair, handlebar mustache?"

The green dude mumbled angrily at the druid.

"He sold me a weathervane—a crappy weathervane!"

"Adrayen means 'Lord of the Dreja.' He is an ancient evil force who has declared himself the Dreja King. No one knows for sure exactly what he is, but some think that he was once one of the gods, now cursed and fallen into darkness.

"Most people thought Adrayen was a myth or a legend until a few thousand years ago when many of the Dreja started to unite and attack as an organized army; something that had never happened before. You see, the Dreja were, until that time, just petty, selfish, chaotic monsters like Ajii who respected nothing but power greater than their own."

"Adrayen is more powerful than any of the Dreja?"

"Yes. And to distinguish his followers from common Dreja, Adrayen dubbed them his knights and gifted them with powerful magic. Arvek is a Knight of Adrayen—one of his four lieutenants, in fact."

"I was a knight under a great king once," the druid said. "I was fired cuz he saw my unique blend of skills and leadership ability as a threat to his throne. That, and I kept 'stealing from the treasury' and 'hitting on the queen.' Pfft, ingrates."

I ignored the druid, which I was learning was usually the best response to his ramblings.

Back to Arvek.

Thinking of the pale man with long hair and vampire teeth made me feel sick. "So what's Adrayen want with this crystal?"

"It's called a Crystal of Destiny." Darius sounded like he was correcting me.

"Then, what's the Crystal of Destiny?" I sniffed and wiped my nose on my sleeve. I'd finally stopped crying, but I was still stuffy.

"There are four, actually. Each one is said to contain a portion of the magic the gods used to create the universe. One holds the power over space, one over time, another creation, and one the power of chaos.

"Each on their own can grant the holder a tremendous amount of power, but if someone were to claim all four..." Darius paused and I caught a tremor in his voice when he said, "it would make that person a god."

"Like Santa Clause?" Bruno asked.

Darius's angry frown returned and he glared at Bruno. "Adrayen is a tyrant and a monster who has already conquered nearly half the worlds in the cosmos and that is just with the two crystals he has." He turned back to look at me. "Those worlds that were once places of life and light have now become wastelands of darkness and death. Imagine what he would do to all existence with the omnipotence of a god!"

"Heh, impotence," the druid snickered.

"Omnipotence!" Darius snapped. "It means all powerful!"

"I watched Arvek open a portal to Earth, so I could see my mom," I said, suddenly making the connection. "Adrayen has the Crystal of Space, doesn't he?"

"And the Crystal of Chaos. Using a magic that is beyond the understanding of any magician now living, Adrayen is able to share the crystal's powers with his most loyal followers."

"So what's the Crystal of Chaos' power?" I asked, not sure I really wanted to know.

"My father and I come from a world called Talaria, a planet not unlike your Earth, save the people there use magic where you rely on technology. Because my world was renowned for training magicians, Adrayen deemed Talaria a threat."

"What did he do?"

Darius got quiet. "He sent the sorceress Vordra, one of his four lieutenants, and she drew on the Crystal of Chaos to..." He breathed in deep.

"What?" I asked.

"Suffice it to say," Darius said, "my world is gone."

"Oh," was all I could say.

Look, I've never been good at offering sympathy. In fact, once, when my third grade teacher's mother died, the substitute teacher made a sympathy card for all of us to sign and write little messages of comfort. While other kids wrote things like *I'm sorry for your loss,* or *Your mother is in Heaven now,* I wrote: *It sucks that your mom died.* That was the day I learned to use white-out.

"Now you have a small idea of what we're up against, and why you can't give my father's crystal to Arvek."

"What do you mean *your father's* crystal?"

"Long ago the gods chose four champions to safeguard the Crystals of Destiny and keep them separate. Each champion was magically bonded to their assigned crystal and charged with its protection. These champions and their successors were called Destiny Keepers. My father, Lobo, was the latest in a long line of keepers of the Crystal of Time."

It hit me and I blurted out, "He passed the Crystal of Time to me, didn't he?"

"Yes."

"But he didn't give me a crystal."

Darius shook his head. "I'm not sure how he did it, but he did."

"No. It's a mistake." I really really wanted it to be a mistake. I wanted Darius to be wrong. But most of all I just wanted to go home.

Darius turned to stare off into the dark. "You have flashes of precognition?"

"I don't know what that means," I said.

Darius turned back and looked me right in the eyes, almost like he was expecting them to start glowing or something. "You see things in visions before they happen, don't you?"

I didn't answer.

"Well?"

I looked away from his intense stare. "Yeah. Sometimes."

"That's a power the keepers of The Crystal of Time had, one of many."

"I can predict things after they happen!" Bruno bragged. Then he added, "Well, if someone explains them to me a couple of times."

"But why give the crystal to me?!"

"As best as I can guess, he had a vision of his impending death, and passed you the bond before he died so it would stay hidden and Adrayen wouldn't be able to just snatch it up. See, the bond masks the magic of the crystal, which otherwise would shine like a sun to anyone trained in the arcane arts. Also, no one but a crystal's keeper can touch it."

I shook my head. "So why didn't Arvek just kill me and go get it himself? Why does he need me to get it?"

"Maybe he's just really lazy," the druid snorted.

Bruno slapped the druid upside the back of his head and said, "You're dumb!"

"Owww..." The druid glared at Bruno as he rubbed the back of his skull.

"I'm certain Adrayen doesn't want to risk one of his servants bonding a Crystal of Destiny themselves, else they try to challenge him. So, to avoid this, he needs Arvek to bring you before him. Also, Arvek doesn't *know* where the crystal is hidden."

"But *he* sent us here!"

"He found out that Iskarin was the world where my father hid the crystal. Beyond that he has no idea. He assigned you a guide so that he could have an inside man to spy on you, and then alert him when you found the crystal. He expected you to lead the way."

"But I don't know where it is!" I wanted to start crying again, but held back my tears.

"Keepers of Destiny have an innate ability to sense the location of their crystal when separated from it." Darius removed his pack and set it on the ground. "Tell me, how did you feel about the direction this dullard was leading you?"

"Hey! Bruno wasn't leading him, I was!" The druid threw a thumb at his chest.

"Yes, I know," Darius said.

Now that I thought about it, I had felt really nervous about the way the druid was taking us. It wasn't normal worry, but felt kinda like those times when you know something bad is going to happen, or something someone is telling you is just not true. Mom said it was my conscience warning me, like when Jiminy Cricket would tell Pinocchio when he was doing something wrong, except I wasn't a possessed talking puppet. Man that was a creepy movie!

Darius was right, though. The feeling of wrongness had gotten worse the closer we got to Zombieville.

"Concentrate," Darius said. "Can you sense its direction?"

I closed my eyes and focused real hard. For a moment nothing happened, then I gasped when something yanked on my chest. "It's that way," I pointed south.

"That's the right direction." He knelt on the ground and began pulling a bedroll from his pack. "See, I know where the crystal is hidden, and can take you to it faster than Arvek expects. After we retrieve it, you will pass the bond to me and I will take my rightful place as keeper of the Crystal of Time."

"Wait, why do I need to go with you?" I asked. "Can't I just pass the bond to you like Lobo did to me?"

Darius shook his head. "Like I said, I'm not sure how my father did what he did. It's not supposed to be possible."

"Why?"

Darius rolled out his sleeping bag. "Because passing the bond normally requires that both the old keeper and the new keeper touch the crystal."

I waited for him to say more, but when he didn't I asked the question that'd been nagging at me during our entire conversation. "So what happens to me after I give you the crystal? How are Bruno and I supposed to get back to our world?"

Darius sighed. "If I had the Crystal of Space, it would be a simple matter. Unfortunately, all I can do is take you back to the Crossroads."

"What?!" I shouted. "Can't you do something to help us?"

"I have no idea how my father found a bridge to your world. It's a place that outsiders rarely travel to. And I'm not as powerful as Ajii—my magic can't tear a hole in space-time."

"So we're stuck?"

"I'm afraid so," Darius said. "I'm sorry."

12

DEAL WITH THE DEVIL

Even though I was pretty upset, running for two hours straight had completely worn me out, so sleep came quickly. But it wasn't the black sleep of exhaustion I'd expected. I actually had some unusually vivid dreams. The first was of me standing on stage in front of a crowd of thousands. They were cheering for me and a man with a microphone was clapping. Someone handed me a bouquet of roses, and placed a tiara on my head. I looked down to see I was wearing an expensive looking, shiny, strapless, blue dress. I touched my lips and my fingers came away with red lipstick.

"Hooray for Thomas!" the man with the microphone shouted. "The most beautiful woman of all!"

The crowd erupted into a loud cheer, standing and furiously clapping. I glanced around the stage, feeling super embarrassed. Behind me stood a row of gorgeous women, all dressed in fine gowns. None of them were smiling. They all looked angry that I'd won the contest instead of them. One pointed at me and screamed, "Get her!"

Normally a guy my age would love a dream about being chased by beauty pageant girls, but this was anything but exciting. I broke left and ran to get off stage but tripped over the six-inch high heels I was wearing. I kicked off the shoes and scrambled up, but was only able to take five steps before one of the angry babes grabbed me by the hair and pulled me backward. I went down again, falling flat on my back. I looked up and found myself surrounded by angry beauty queens. They started kicking me, and I raised my arms to shield my face.

Miss Alabama pushed her way to the front of the chaos, proclaiming that her stage talent was to rip someone's heart out in three quick wrist movements. Oddly, even such a terrifying threat sounded kinda cute when said in that southern accent.

The dream changed and I found myself standing on the dirty street of what looked like a town right out of an old western film. Come to think of it, it looked like Zombieville, only not run down. I no longer had on the blue dress, but instead wore a cowboy hat, leather vest with a silver star pinned to it, and jeans held up by a belt with a really big buckle. Two holstered revolvers hung at my hips.

I heard the green dude gibbering and looked up to find the creature standing about thirty feet in front of me. He still wore his sunglasses, but his black hat had been replaced by a sombrero, and he had a handlebar mustache just above where his mouth should have been. When I saw the two guns hanging in holsters at the green dude's sides, I immediately knew what I had to do.

"I'm going to give you a chance to come quietly, Cactus Pete!" My voice came out with an exaggerated Texas drawl.

The creature replied with a defiant sounding string of gibberish.

"I ain't given you no second chance." I spat on the ground.

Again the green dude responded angrily.

"Then I'm taking you out!" I hesitated for a moment, noticing for the first time that I had an audience consisting entirely of emperor penguins and a brunette in an old west style dress. Her hair was curled in tight ringlets, and she smiled at me. It was Sherry Allen, a girl I'd had a crush on since the third grade.

I smiled and tipped my hat to her. "Ma'am," I said and Sherry giggled and waved at me.

That gave me courage and I turned back to face the green dude. "You ready to meet yer maker, Cactus Pete?"

The green dude's gibbering response had a threatening tone to it.

"THEN DRAW!"

My hands went to the white handles of my six-shooters. The green dude made a desperate squealing noise as he looked helplessly at the guns hanging at his sides. Without arms, he couldn't draw. This didn't stop me however, and in one quick motion I drew and fired two shots. The green dude babbled in pain and collapsed to the ground, causing a loud cheer to erupt from the crowd of on-looking penguins. I turned to see Sherry Allen lifting the bottom of her bell shaped dress as she stepped off the boardwalk and rushed toward me.

She threw her arms around me and stared up into my eyes. "Thomas, you're my hero!" She smiled, flashing me her adorable dimples. Seeing those always made my stomach flutter. Then she raised up on her tiptoes and kissed me. I closed my eyes and kissed her back. It was even more awesome than my recurring dream of Sherry and I winning the Super Bowl together.

Unfortunately, when I opened my eyes, Sherry was gone, replaced by a disgusting, tan-furred llama. I quickly pulled away and began spitting out llama slobber. The animal grunted and trotted away. I wanted to puke, but the horror of making out with a slobbery llama faded when I found myself dressed in my gym clothes and standing on my school's running track. Standing next to me, focused and getting ready for a foot-race, were the druid, the green dude, and Bruno. I quickly put my foot forward and got ready to race.

"On your marks!" a voice shouted.

I glanced to the side where Darius stood dressed in a referee's striped shirt. He held a pistol high above his head.

"Get set!" For some reason Darius lowered the pistol and aimed it at us.

"Wait!" I shouted. "Darius, what are you doing?"

"Go!" He fired.

The druid and green dude took off down the track, but Bruno was hit by Darius's shot and collapsed face down onto the red pavement.

"Bruno!" I ran to kneel next to him. I rolled the big kid over and instantly knew he was dead.

"No!" I screamed. And then Bruno was gone and I was holding C.J.'s stone head. The scene had also changed from the school's running track to Caesar's Palace. "I'm so sorry, C.J."

I started to cry but stopped when I heard laughing all around me. It echoed throughout the empty courtyard. Then it was coming from behind me. I turned to find Ajii staring down at me, the holes in his smooth white mask completely black. I dropped C.J.'s head and scrambled away from him.

"Hello Thomas." Ajii's voice wasn't in my head like before, and it was deep, not at all the high pitched screechy sound the Dreja had made.

"You're not Ajii!!" I shouted. "You're not real!"

"You are both right and wrong," Ajii laughed. "I am not that crazed Dreja Lobo helped you kill. I am, however, very very real."

"Who are you?" I put enough space between us that I felt safe standing up.

"You're no fool, boy," Ajii said. "You know who I am."

The voice definitely belonged to someone else.

"Adrayen?" I guessed.

A crack appeared in Ajii's white mask, just where his mouth would've been. It broke open forming a hideous smile with nothing behind it but blackness. "Yes," the monster said, though its new mouth didn't move.

"Why are you here?" My voice shook.

"I have come to ensure that you will honor our accord."

"You want me to give you the Crystal of Time," I said.

"Yes, for which I will send you and your friend home to Earth."

"Darius said that you're evil." I continued to slowly back away. "He said you've destroyed entire worlds."

Adrayen chuckled. "Thomas, you are too clever to be chained by the dogma of such black and white thinking. Evil is a subjective term. What one may call evil, another might call necessary for the greater good."

"That's not what I learned in Sunday school," I said, now trying to use sarcasm to sound brave.

It didn't work.

"Believe what you want." Adrayen's smile was suddenly a frown. "It all comes to the same; you have something that I want, and I am the only one who can send you home."

"If Lobo found a way to Earth, then so can I."

"Perhaps you may, but even if you do, it will take years, maybe even decades. You could be a very old man by the time you find a bridge that will take you home."

Suddenly we were standing in a cemetery. I saw an old man looking down at a headstone. I knew the old man was me, and the name on the headstone was Mom's name.

"No!" I shouted.

"You think you've known loneliness in an alien world? Such will be nothing compared to the emptiness you will experience should you return to a home that has long forgotten you."

Tears poured down my cheeks as I shook my head. "I don't want that."

"Of course not," Adrayen said. "And you won't have to endure it, if you give me the Crystal of Time. I even have the power to wipe your memory of all that has happened, so that you can go on living your life in blissful ignorance."

Again I felt like I was standing in front of the door to Ajii's prison, scared and just wanting to do whatever it took to get away. That's probably why Adrayen appeared in the form of Ajii. He really was a master of manipulation.

The older version of me was gone now, and so I took his place kneeling in front of Mom's headstone. "Lobo died to keep you from getting the crystal."

"What do you owe Lobo? He kidnapped you, put you in danger, and left you stranded on an alien world."

It was all true. Lobo had abandoned me, just like my dad. I suddenly felt anger mix in with my terror. This was all too much for me.

"I'll do it," I whispered. "I'll give you the crystal."

Adrayen's smile was suddenly back. "You have made the right choice, child."

The guilt stinging my chest told me I hadn't.

Then Adrayen was gone, and his voice again came at me from all directions. "When you get the crystal, speak these words: Sala trose, vorsik Adrayen, and I will find you."

And then his voice was gone too, but the words weren't. They burned into my memory and echoed in my head.

"Sala trose, vorsik Adrayen," I said to myself. I didn't know what they actually meant, but for me they translated into *I'm a selfish coward.*

13

THE ROAD AHEAD

"Thomas!" Someone called my name.

"Thomas!" they said a little louder.

I woke to find Darius standing over me. I gasped and sat up. Darius crouched down and put a hand on my shoulder. "Are you ok?"

I stared at him, guilt and fear making me want to cry and confess everything, but I just nodded. His eyes narrowed at me for just a second before he smiled and patted me on the back. That flash of suspicion made me nervous, and I started worrying that maybe Darius knew I'd just promised to betray him.

"It's time to get moving."

Darius walked away to start gathering his things, and I glanced around our camp. It'd been cold and Darius hadn't let us build a fire. Bruno and I had the blankets we'd bought before leaving The Crossroads, but the druid was curled up in ball on the ground shaking. It made me kinda feel sorry for him. The green dude hadn't moved all night. He'd just stayed upright in the middle of camp, watching us, which kinda creeped me out, actually.

"I'm hungry!" Bruno yawned.

"Well, I hope you brought some food with you, because I packed light in order to chase you down." Darius packed his bedroll into a satchel and then drank from a weird leather bag shaped like a horn.

I dug a small loaf of bread out of my pack, broke it in half, and handed the bigger piece to Bruno. He grabbed it, then snatched my half, and shoved them both into his mouth. I didn't say anything. The memory of Adrayen's last words still echoed in my head making me too sick to be hungry.

"Where are we going?" I finally asked Darius.

"Well, first we need to get out of the Necrotic Expanse."

"The what?"

"Zombieville, and the surrounding vicinity, is called the Necrotic Expanse," Darius explained. "It's cursed ground that turns anyone who dies on it into some kind of undead monster."

"Oh." I looked at the druid still curled up in a ball and shivering. All the feelings of pity I had toward him were gone as I realized just how close I'd come to spending eternity as a zombie.

Darius continued, "The quickest way to get out of the Necrotic Expanse will be to cut through Echo Wood on the south. After we're out, we'll turn east and take the Jora road to an island a few miles off the coast in the Sea of Ages. That's where my father hid the Crystal of Time." Darius stared at the horizon. "It is a highly traveled path we follow, but we don't have time to cut cross-country. We need to get the Crystal of Time as quickly as possible, transfer its bond to me, and get back to The Crossroads before Arvek comes looking for us." Darius dug in his bag and pulled out two apples. He tossed one to me, then stood and took a bite of the other.

He drank again from his water bag and then walked over to where the druid slept on the ground. Darius took another bite of his apple, and then turned his water bag over so it poured directly onto the druid's face.

"Wha-what-cold?" The druid sputtered. His eyes snapped open and he sat up, wildly rubbing his face with the sleeve of his black cloak.

It was mean, but I couldn't help but laugh, not after what that jerk had put us through. And I couldn't be sure, but it sounded like the green dude was laughing too.

"Get up!" Darius ordered.

The druid lifted his head, frowning as he apparently realized what just happened. "How dare you treat the crown prince of Dathak this way?"

"You're a drifter," Darius said. "And that's not a real place."

"It could be!" the druid protested.

"I said, get up!" Darius threatened to pour more water on him.

"Ok, ok, ok!" The druid stood and brushed himself off. "Sheesh!"

Bruno turned to the druid. "You scream in your sleep."

"Not always!" the druid said in a defensive tone. "Sometimes I'm told I merely sob quietly."

Darius stoppered his water bag and hung it at his belt. "We're going." He turned and stepped away from the druid.

"And so our quest begins!" The druid announced.

"Yay, quest!" Bruno clapped.

The green dude made a happy noise.

"No!" Darius spun around. "After we get out of the Necrotic Expanse, you half-wits can go back to The Crossroads. I have enough to be concerned about without having to babysit you three!"

"No," I said. "Bruno comes with me."

"You're not in charge here, *kid*." Darius stared at me, and I have to confess, I was very intimidated; even more so than I am by circus clowns. But I'd treated Bruno badly since I met him, and I wasn't about to do it again. Besides, I needed to do something good to help make my guilt go away.

"Yeah, but you need me, Darius." I folded my arms. "And Bruno's my friend. If you won't take him, then I won't go with you!"

Darius stared at me for a long moment and then gave me a sharp nod. "Fine!" He pointed at the druid and the green dude. "But those two only come with us as far as the Expanse boundary. Where they go from there is not our problem."

"You need me too!" The druid angrily protested. "You'll never find the crystal without a guide!"

Darius dropped his satchel, stepped toward the druid, and grabbed the front of his robes.

"You," he said through clenched teeth, "are a fool and a liar, and I won't let you or your green pet blob endanger the cause of the guardians with your self-serving stupidity." Darius held the druid until the man nodded his acceptance. He released the druid and went back to his pack, fished in it, and drew out a pair of long knives.

"What're those for?" I asked, suddenly worried Darius was going to use them on the druid.

"They are for you." Darius held them out to me, handles first.

I stared at them. "I'm not a fighter."

"Which is why I have placed an enchantment on these daggers. While you wield them in battle, you'll have grace and skill beyond your normal abilities. It's an easy spell, one that my people used to help young warriors learn to fight."

Great, magic training wheels.

I took the daggers. "You're a magician?"

Darius handed me a belt with empty sheathes hanging from it, then slung his satchel onto his back and began adjusting the shoulder straps. "The last Talarian magician in the universe."

"Was Lobo a magician too?" I belted the empty sheathes to my hips and slid the daggers inside. I gotta say, it made me look really cool.

Darius shook his head. "Father preferred using magic weapons to casting spells. He trained me somewhat in the ways of a swordsman." Darius belted on Lobo's sword so that it hung in a sheath at his left hip. "However, I ended up gravitating more toward the arcane arts."

"Ajii said I had magic." I'd been wondering about this for a while and was glad for the chance to ask.

"Because The Crystals of Destiny are the source of all

magic, while you're bonded to one you can access the arcane."

"So I could learn to cast spells?" The idea excited me.

"Probably, if you had a decade to learn and someone to teach you."

"I could be your mentor!" The druid exclaimed, before taking a step back at a glare from Darius.

Maybe that could be my way home, I thought. *Maybe I could learn how to open a portal back to Earth.* Ajii had been able to open a portal to The Crossroads. But no. I was going to give the crystal to Darius, and when that happened, I'd lose my magic. I thought of my nightmare and the deal I'd made with Adrayen. The scene of me kneeling at Mom's grave as an old man drove home the fact that I had no choice but to give the crystal to Adrayen. That didn't make my guilt go away, so I forced it to the back of my mind.

"Come on!" Darius called back. He was already setting out, the green dude gliding along just behind him.

I glanced at Bruno. He smiled and pulled me into another bear hug. "Thanks for standing up for me, Thomas. No one's ever done that before."

I wasn't able to respond until he let me go, and even then I could barely breathe. "No problem," I wheezed.

"Here, Thomas," Bruno said as he pulled something from his pocket. "I want you to have it."

It was the harmonica he'd bought back at the tower-city. I looked at his face and his big smile wouldn't let me refuse it.

"Thanks," I said, and then took the harmonica and slid it in my pocket.

We followed Darius.

"Wait!" the druid yelled from behind us. "You need me! I'm your only hope!"

I glanced back just in time to see the cloaked man turn away from peeing on a tree. He dropped his cloak, tripped, and then looked down at his hands and frowned. He wiped them on the front of his robes and hurried after us.

14

INTO ECHO WOOD

"The Necrotic Expanse," Darius explained as we walked, "is cursed ground that covers dozens of miles. I'm not sure anyone has ever actually mapped its borders." He glanced over his shoulder at the druid. "Because *most* people have the good sense to stay away from it."

The druid looked back to where the green dude glided along. "Yeah!" he said in an accusing tone. "Seriously. Some people..."

The green dude protested with a stream of angry sounding gibberish.

Darius frowned. "There is a river that borders one side of the forest where the undead cannot cross. Most believe that to be at least one part of the boundary."

"How did this land get cursed?" I asked.

"Legend tells of a powerful necromancer—that's a magician who uses black magic to control and communicate with the dead—that built his castle here. His name was Olis, and he was brilliant; so talented that by his magic he was able to prolong his life for hundreds of years. But old age eventually caught up with him, and so in an effort to achieve immortality, he tried to turn himself into what's called a lich. That's a kind of zombie wizard."

"So, what went wrong?" I asked.

"The complex ritual he was performing failed, and instead of turning him into an immortal lich, the spell exploded outward, cursing the land around the castle so that any who died thereon would rise to become some kind of undead monster."

"Not just zombies?"

Darius chuckled. "Unfortunately, there are a lot of different kinds of undead. Zombies are just the most common and least dangerous."

That made me feel cold. What else might we have run into in this place? "So where was the necromancer's castle?"

Darius pointed at the large dark forest we'd been heading toward. "Somewhere inside Echo Wood, though it's sure to be little more than overgrown ruins by now."

I stopped walking. "Wait! This is the center of the Necrotic Expanse?"

Darius glanced back at me. "The fastest way out is to cut straight through the middle."

"Isn't it gonna be full of undead monsters?"

"It is."

The druid came up behind me and laid a hand on my shoulder. "Don't worry, young Thomas. I shall protect you with my..."

I threw off his hand and trotted up to Darius. "Can't we go around?"

Darius stopped and faced me. "We wouldn't be here at all if it wasn't for that black-robed charlatan, or your naïve trust in his lies."

"Do not feel bad Thomas," the druid said quietly. "I forgive you for the mess you've gotten us into."

I wanted to punch him, but my fear overpowered my irritation. "What kind of monsters live in that forest?"

"Live?" Darius chuckled.

"You know what I mean."

"I imagine ghouls, wraiths, skeletons, maybe even a banshee."

"And raccoons?" The druid suddenly sounded nervous.

Darius shot him a disgusted look, but refused to answer. "Look, Thomas, we'll be fine as long as we make it through the forest before nightfall. The undead hate the sun, and hide during the day, even in a thick forest."

I looked up at the sky and found the sun still rising. I resumed walking toward the forest.

Bruno gripped my arm and whispered in a frightened voice, "Did he say there'll be raccoons?"

"Don't worry." I patted Bruno on the back.

Trusting a stranger to lead us had already almost gotten me killed. But Darius seemed legit, and powerful, so I followed him. I'm not sure what I expected, but our trip through Echo Wood wasn't a brisk stroll. Darius made us jog, threatening to leave anyone behind who couldn't keep up. I felt like I was in gym class again.

After about three hours of this, I just plain ran out of steam and stopped to lean against one of the tall pines. Bruno crashed to the ground and lay on his back, heaving. The druid wasn't in much better shape. Of course, the creature that we called the green dude just glided by me as though the furious pace wasn't affecting him at all.

Darius stopped running and stalked back toward us. "What are you doing?!"

"I need a break," I said between gasps. "We all do."

Darius looked at the druid, and then Bruno. Both were sucking air and covered in sweat.

"Just give us fifteen minutes," I begged.

Darius looked up through the forest canopy at the sun now high in the sky. "You have ten." He walked away.

"You have ten," the druid mocked. He sat down on the ground, kicked off his shoes and began rubbing his bare feet. "*I* never made you run yourself to death when *I* was leading you, Thomas. In fact, I never complicated our quest with any of these pointless details like *purpose* or *destination* either."

"No, you just led us into the land of the living dead." I walked away, not giving him a chance to reply with one of his stupid lies.

I found Bruno rolled over on his side reaching for a patch of white mushrooms on the ground with his tongue hanging out like a dog's.

"Don't eat those!"

Bruno jumped and pulled his hand back. "I wasn't going to!"

I folded my arms. "Then what were you doing?"

Bruno sat up, but kept his eyes down like a kid who'd been caught stealing from the cookie jar.

"I was going to use the mushrooms to put on a two minute, Korean, finger-puppet show."

I walked over to the cluster of mushrooms and kicked them apart with one foot. "Do you know how dangerous it is to eat wild mushrooms?"

"I was gonna share with everybody," Bruno said.

"They can kill you! Remember the rats that died from eating those blue mushrooms at The Crossroads?"

"But I'm so hungry!" Bruno whined.

"We'll eat when we're out of the forest."

"Thomas!" Darius called.

"Just hold on a little longer, ok?"

Bruno nodded and I walked away. I passed the druid who looked at Bruno and chuckled.

"What's so funny?" I demanded.

The druid shook his head. "Nothin'"

I looked at Bruno and found him with mushroom caps on his fingertips. He bobbed them up and down at each other, and spoke in a high-pitched language that I'm sure wasn't even close to Korean.

"Don't eat those!" I shouted one more time for good measure.

"SHHH! You're interrupting act two!" Bruno said.

I moved on past the green dude who mumbled something at me, and I tried not to look at him. Although I'd become used to the creature, his ridiculous sunglasses and black hat still kinda creeped me out. Who did he think he was fooling with that lame disguise anyway?

I found Darius overlooking a small ravine. "I need to warn you of something."

"What?"

"Adrayen is powerful in ways even the guardians don't

understand, more so because he has two of the Crystals of Destiny. He may try to communicate with you."

I froze. Did Darius know I'd talked to Adrayen? Was he trying to get me to confess? "What do you mean?" I said trying to sound calm.

Darius turned and looked at me. "He has the power to reach out psychically. I don't know much more than that. I don't think we need to worry too much, not while Arvek thinks we're about his business. But if he should try to contact you..."

"I'll tell you right away." I groaned inside. Had I sounded too eager?

Darius cupped his hands to his mouth and called, "Alright freaks! It's time to move!"

We jogged at a slower pace for the next couple of hours. As fit as he was, I think the running was getting to Darius too. The strange quiet of the forest made it so even little sounds we made echoed loudly through the trees. That's how Echo Wood got its name. It was eerie. I couldn't hear any birds, bugs, or animal noises; probably because every creature in the forest was some kind of zombie.

We jogged on, and it was late into the afternoon by the time I noticed Bruno was missing.

I stopped. "Bruno?" I called. My own voice came back in response. "Bruno?" Still only an echo.

"Why are we stopping?" Darius jogged back to me.

"Bruno!" I double backed a dozen paces, looking through the walls of trees on either side of the path. "Darius, he's gone!"

"Are you sure he just isn't lagging behind?"

I shook my head and looked back to where Bruno should've been. "I think he might've gotten lost."

Darius glanced up at the sky where the sun sat low on the western horizon. "It's almost dusk!"

"You can't leave him, Darius!" I pled.

"Oh, don't waste your time, Thomas," the druid suddenly cut in. "He's probably long dead."

"What're you talking about?"

"You remember those mushrooms you told him not to eat? Well, after the puppet show, which was really quite good I might add. Except for the middle of the second act..."

Darius grabbed the druid by the throat. "He ate them?"

The druid's eyes widened. "Yeah?"

"You saw this and you didn't stop him?"

"And interrupt the curtain call? I would never dare to be so uncouth!"

"Did you see what happened to him after he ate the mushrooms?" I asked.

The druid was starting to struggle for breath, his face turning purple. "He-said-something," he choked out, "about being invited to a tea party-by a family of penguins-and left the trail. It was actually-kinda-funny."

Darius let go of the druid's throat and shoved him so hard that he fell to the ground. He rolled onto his side and started coughing, and sucking air.

"How about I make *you* eat some of those mushrooms and then we'll see just how funny it is!" Darius turned to me. "Those mushrooms cause hallucinations. If Bruno went after what he saw, he could be anywhere."

"What do we do?"

"Night is coming! We have to get out of the forest before sundown or we're *all* dead!"

"I can't leave him!" I said. "He's my friend!"

Darius's jaw tightened.

"Please," I begged.

Darius gave a sharp nod and broke into a run back the way we'd come. I followed, adrenaline washing away my worn-out feeling and numbing the pain in my legs. I didn't look back, but I heard the druid and green dude arguing, I knew they would follow.

Darius ran for nearly an hour, not jogged, but ran. Even in full panic mode, I had a hard time keeping up. He stopped when he came upon large sneaker tread prints—Bruno's tracks. He knelt, waved a hand over the print in the soft ground and the tracks suddenly lit up with a bright blue glow. Like falling dominos, the next set of tracks lit up, and then the next, and the next until we had a glowing trail leading off into the trees. I wished I could do that. *I* would've been the hide and seek champ at stuck-up Billy Tanner's eighth birthday party! I guess it wouldn't have mattered since no one else was playing, or at least no one came looking for *me*. Unless you counted the police.

Darius checked the sky again. It was almost dusk. "Come on!" he ordered, and we began to follow the glowing trail.

15

DEAD CENTER

We followed the trail of glowing blue sneaker prints up a hill, and Darius froze when we came to the top. Bruno's shining tracks led down the other side of the hill and disappeared into a gigantic ravine. At the bottom of the ravine was an old castle. It was overgrown with thorny vines, and one of its four spires had collapsed, but otherwise it was whole. I didn't even need to ask Darius what this was. I knew.

"What's...that place?" the druid said in between pants.

"Olis's castle," I answered quietly.

"Who?"

Darius spun. "Don't you *ever* listen?" he hissed at the druid. "This is the very *center* of the Necrotic Expanse! And that castle is sure to be filled with zombies, skeletons, wraiths, maybe even a vampire!"

"And Bruno went in there? Well, that was stupid," he scoffed.

Darius shot his hand out, grabbed the druid by the collar of his robe, and hurled him down the hill. The druid rolled and somersaulted, crying out whenever he hit a rock or tree branch. Eventually he disappeared beneath the thick grass.

"Come on," Darius ordered, and then began running down the hill.

We found the druid at the bottom of the hill picking brambles out of his hair. He opened his mouth to say something but I locked eyes with him and shook my head in warning. He closed his mouth, dusted himself off, and stood.

We followed the glowing prints through thick underbrush until we came to an old stone road. It was broken up with plants growing in between the flagstones, and was completely buried by dirt in some places. The trail of glowing prints followed the road, and so we ran on.

By the time we reached the gate that led to the castle's courtyard, the sun had completely set. No undead monsters had made their appearance yet, but the air felt like it had changed. It didn't smell like plants, dirt, and trees anymore, it smelled like rotting meat. It felt thicker too, like some invisible hand was pressing down on my shoulders.

The castle gate was little more than bent rusted bars hanging on a frame bolted to a stone archway. Bruno's glowing prints led straight into the courtyard, but stopped in front of an empty fountain. There was a flash of light, and suddenly the hero blade was in Darius's hand. I took that to mean I should pull out my daggers, which I did. When my skin touched their handles, Darius's spell took effect and I felt an electric shock, not painful, but it definitely came from the daggers.

Darius led the way into the courtyard, and I followed. I hadn't gotten more than ten steps in when I noticed the druid lingering outside the gate. He was blocking the green dude from entering by shifting his step every time the creature tried to pass him. It reminded me of watching an NBA player go man to man with someone on the opposing team.

"What are you doing?" I tried to whisper and shout at the same time, but it came out sounding like a hiss.

"Someone needs to guard our retreat," the druid said. "I volunteer and nominate Green to be my companion. You can reward me for my bravery later."

Darius scoffed. "Let the coward stay outside. It's not really any safer. And we might get lucky and something will eat them."

I forced a nervous chuckle, hoping Darius was joking. We continued on without the druid and the green dude and followed Bruno's steps up to the dry fountain. It was tall, with three tiers and was topped by the statue of an angel. From the vines growing in the basin, and the cracks in the stone, it was clear the fountain hadn't seen water in a very long time.

"His tracks end here," Darius said as he walked around the fountain.

"Where did he go?" I glanced up at the castle. In the dark against the rising moon, it looked like something out of a Halloween decoration.

"Something must've taken him."

"Like what?"

Darius stared at the stone ground and shook his head. "I don't know. There're other tracks here—inhuman tracks."

I looked hard where Darius was focusing his attention and saw what looked like the footprints of an elephant. Even the stone inside the prints was cracked like whatever made them was very big and very heavy. The monstrous tracks led away from the fountain and into the castle.

"He's inside," I said.

The tightening of Darius's jaw scared me. I waited for him to say something, but a distant moaning wail from somewhere in the surrounding woods distracted me. It was long, low, and sent a chill through my entire body. The sound of footsteps from behind made me spin and bring up my knives. The druid ran up to us, his eyes wide and face white, the green dude gliding just behind him.

"As noble a cause as guarding the gate is," he said. "I think you're going to need my heroism more in there. So it is with much reluctance that I give up all hope of gate guarding glory to accompany you into that castle of darkness and unknown horrors."

"And your change of heart had absolutely nothing to do with that ghostly scream we all just heard?" I said.

The druid blinked owlishly. "What ghostly scream?"

I turned back to Darius. He was still staring at the castle, his brow furrowed as though he were trying to make a hard decision. "Darius!" I said. "You're not going to leave him, are you?"

Finally, Darius sighed, and shook his head. "Come on." He ran forward, Lobo's sword held up, and ready.

The double doors on the front of the castle were tall—like twenty feet or something. The left door was shut, and the right hung open on its bottom hinge only. Darius conjured a ball of light, like the one he made in Zombieville, but smaller and dimmer. It cast a soft white halo around us for about five feet, but it was enough to show me that the inside of the castle was just as old and decrepit as the outside.

There were cracks in the walls and floor. Stone blocks from one of the walls were scattered all over the ground, and it was so cold I could see my breath. I expected zombies to start moaning and charge at us, but the castle's foyer was empty. Honestly, that was almost worse than it being full of monsters.

The druid, wild-eyed and sweating, clamped a hand down on my upper arm so hard that it hurt. I yanked it free and shoved him away. "Watch it!" I hissed.

"You looked as though you were in need of comfort," he whispered. But it was clear from the look on his face that he was far more terrified than I was. Pathetic, considering he was an adult and I was just a kid.

"Just don't touch me," I said.

"But Green is too slippery. Who am I supposed to hold onto?"

I didn't answer, but moved to walk closer to Darius. We followed the giant elephant-like tracks up four flights of wide stone steps and up to the castle's third level. There, red tattered curtains blew into the hall from the wind coming in through broken windows. Still we didn't encounter any evil things, although I did have that feeling that we were being watched. You know the one where your skin prickles, and the back of your head and neck feels warm? I saw movement out of the corners of my eyes; dark shadows darting almost into full view before flitting away.

I had finally gotten my fear and imagination under

control when Darius ruined it by saying, "We're being watched."

Great.

Fighting every instinct telling me to run, I kept going, gripping the handles of my daggers a little tighter. There was a rug over the stone floor that ran the entire length of the hall. It was red like the curtains, and in worse shape with tears along the sides, and holes in the middle. We came to an open door at the end of a long hall through which we could see the flickering of yellow light. Darius cautiously entered the room first, and then motioned for me to follow. When I got inside, I found that the room was lit with candles placed in brackets all along the wall.

The chamber was huge, almost as big as the foyer on the ground floor, and it was so tall that I couldn't see the ceiling. In the center was a round stone altar set on top of a platform. On that altar lay Bruno, surrounded by six figures wearing black cloaks. They were chanting something low and ominous. Bruno was awake, his eyes wide, and his hands and feet bound by cords.

Darius and I moved along the wall, trying to get into a better position from which to strike. *My* only experience with fighting and strategy came from playing Call of Duty, and I was always the guy who died first in that game. So, I guess you could say I was more than a little worried that this wouldn't go well.

"They can't know we're here until we're right on top of them," Darius whispered. "If we..."

"My brethren!" the druid whispered and motioned excitedly at the cloaked figures surrounding the altar. "I can go among them, blend in, and liberate Bruno from the inside!"

"That's the dumbest thing you've ever sugges..." I trailed off as the druid ran forward.

"By the grace of the four powers!" Darius growled. "He's going to get us *all* killed!"

It was too late to stop him. The druid was already walking up to the platform and altar. "Brothers!" he called and waved. "Tis a perfect night for a sacrifice, wouldn't you agree?"

The figures all turned to face us and I froze when I saw what had been concealed under their hoods—skulls. They looked like they could be the grim reaper's cousins with their skull faces and bone hands. But instead of wielding soul stealing scythes, each held an ornate dagger.

The druid squealed and ran back toward us.

"Ah crumpet," I said, proud of myself for not saying crap.

The six cloaked creatures broke their circle and glided toward us, quiet, and terrifying. I guess I expected to hear their bones rattling like a cartoon skeleton I saw once, but they didn't make any kind of noise. For some reason that made them even scarier.

Darius stretched out his hand, pointed at one of the reapers, and yelled "Kaji!" The cloaked skeleton burst into flames and began screeching. Darius charged forward. He whirled into the remaining five reapers, Lobo's sword tearing through cloak and shattering bone.

I took a step forward and my hand shot up like it was possessed. Before I knew it, I had cocked back and thrown one of my daggers. It spun blade over handle before hitting one of the reapers in its empty eye socket. It screeched as it fell apart, its bones landing in a heap beneath its black cloak.

"Thomas help!" Bruno shouted.

Shoving down my sizable fear—we're talking like the two-hundred toilet paper roll extended family pack size, ya know the kind you'd find in those warehouse stores that require a club card to get into—I charged toward the altar. I figured out long ago that if I sung a certain song I learned in kindergarten, I was able to keep calm whenever I was afraid.

"The farmer's dog lay on the floor..." I sang as quiet as I could, "...and Bingo was name-oh..."

Again, like it had a mind of its own, my hand shot down and pulled the dagger from the eye-socket of the reaper I'd destroyed as I ran past it.

"...B-I-N-G-O, B-I-N-G-O..."

One of the monsters came at me, but holding both daggers out, I spun tearing through its cloak with my first blade, and smashing its ribcage into dust with the second. Like the first reaper, it fell into a pile of cloth and bones.

"...and Bingo was his name-oh!"

The enchanted knives Darius had given me were the most awesome-est training wheels I'd ever used. Like my real training wheels, I never wanted to take these off. Um, which of course I had to. I mean what twelve-year-old still uses training wheels? Pfft, not me. That's for darn sure...

Anyway, by the time I reached the altar Darius had destroyed the remaining reapers. As with his father, the hero blade made him faster and stronger and he'd torn through the monsters like a tornado.

I stopped singing as I ran up to Bruno. He was crying.

"I'm sorry, Thomas. I know I messed up, but the mushrooms were just so yummy! And then the penguins invited me to tea, and the leprechaun said he'd show me his pot of gold, but he wasn't talking about gold coins, he…"

"It's ok, Bruno," I said, and used one of my daggers to cut free his hands and feet.

They came apart easily, something that must've been part of Darius's magic, because they looked to be made of something stronger than rope. I held one of the cut cords up to examine it.

"What are these made of?"

"Human entrails," a voice rasped from the back of the room.

The temperature dropped from "I-need-a-jacket-cold" to "I'm-going-to-die-of-hypothermia-freezing." Darius raised his sword in front of him, ready for another fight.

Bruno started to cry again. "It's the ghost of my hamster, Mr. Wiggles. I knew I shouldn't have tried to teach him how to snorkel in the bathtub."

"Darius?" I called. But he ignored me.

A vision flashed in my mind, so quick that I didn't have time to process it before a figure stepped into view. For a field trip once, my second-grade class had gone to the university to see an exhibit of Egyptian mummies. Many of them had their faces unwrapped, and I remember the shriveled skin, missing noses, and black holes where their eyes should've been—I couldn't sleep for weeks. This creature looked like that, except intense points of green light burned in his empty eye sockets, and he was dressed in a nice looking red robe. He also wore rings on his fingers, and was holding a book under one arm.

"It's like catgut, but made from humans," the creature laughed. It was a horrible sound, like a laughing snake.

Darius charged forward, but the monster lazily pointed at him and Darius froze. He looked like he was trying to move—his eyebrows crinkled and his jaw tightened. After a few seconds, he was hurled back by an invisible force. He slammed into the stone wall, dropping Lobo's sword, and slumping to the ground. I didn't know if he was knocked out or dead, but he didn't move.

The druid tried to run, but the mummy-man flicked his wrist and he fell flat on his face. The green dude whipped out a tentacle, but was hurled up into the air so fast that his hat flew off. He came down in a splat, sunglasses losing a lens as they clattered across the stone floor.

The creature turned to look at me, and my arms and legs wouldn't move. I could still talk though. "Who are you?" I forced out in a shaky voice.

"I am Olis," mummy-man said. "This is my castle, and you are trespassing here."

Olis? It was the wizard whose failed spell had created the Necrotic Expanse. "I thought you died," I said through chattering teeth.

Olis rasped another hideous laugh. "I did die, child. That was sort of the point." He stepped closer to me. "But if you're referring to the legend that my spell failed, and that this land is cursed by accident, then you are mistaken. Though I have encouraged that fallacy as best I can. I find it an effective lure to unsuspecting or foolish travelers, which has provided me with a steady stream of recruits for my army."

Bruno summoned his silver club and stood in front of me, but Olis waved and he was thrown to the side.

"Bruno!"

Olis stepped in close, and looked me straight in the eye. I was surprised he didn't stink like the rotting zombies of Zombieville. It was a weird thing to notice at the moment. His glowing green eyes stared into mine and he smiled. Some of his teeth were missing, and I didn't see a tongue.

"I sensed you coming from a long way off," Olis said. He stepped back and looked down at Bruno. "Your Gigas infant here was most helpful in luring you into my lair. Once he'd partaken of those Psilocybin, he heard my call and came straight here."

"What are you talking about?" I managed through chattering teeth. I wasn't sure if it was from the sudden cold in the room, or fear. Probably both. I was just glad I'd kept control of my bladder—mostly.

"You have something I want," Olis said. "And if you bring it to me, I'm willing to let your friends live."

"Thomas, no!" I heard Darius groan and I was glad to know he was still alive. "Better we all die!"

"Oh, you could die, but that wouldn't be the end," Olis said. "You would join the ranks of my army and, when the time is right, would march with me to conquer the Crossroads."

"Adrayen would come after you!" Darius shouted. "Do you want that?"

Olis glanced at Darius. "And what is my old friend going

to do? Kill me?" He broke into more rasping laughter and then grabbed me by the throat with one of his boney hands. "You will bring me the crystal you are bound to, or watch as I torture your friends to death, and then raise them as children of the night and force them to torture you!"

He wasn't choking me, but there was some pressure on my throat that hurt. I started to cry and thought of Mom. I'm glad I didn't actually call out for her, but I wanted to. I didn't know what to do. If I agreed to Olis's demands, he'd let us live for now, but what then? I couldn't bring him the crystal. Would Arvek even let me? A part of me suggested that I could still make it home if I abandoned Bruno, Darius, and the others and I'm ashamed to admit I considered it for a moment.

"Well, boy?" Olis's smile was gone now. "Choose, or I start making them scream."

I don't think I've ever felt so desperate. I thought about trying to call out for the hero blade on the floor, but I knew that wouldn't work. In fact, Darius hadn't explained to me how he called it. That meant I'd probably just be yelling "Jackpot" like a moron.

I closed my eyes, and felt something I hadn't felt before. It's hard to describe, but it was like my mind opened up, and I was connected to everything. It was kinda like finding the universe's Wi-Fi hotspot.

Not knowing what I was doing, I focused on that feeling with all of my desperate will.

Time stopped.

I'm not saying that to sound dramatic, I mean it literally froze. Like I had paused a videogame. Everything went quiet,

Olis stood still like some kind of horror movie prop, and all the flames of the candles in wall brackets stopped flickering. I pulled free of Olis's boney hand and stumbled back. The lich didn't move. He just stood in the same position.

Bruno got up and stepped over to me, keeping his wide eyes on Olis. "What'd you do Thomas?"

"I don't know."

Darius launched to his feet, Lobo's sword in hand. He charged Olis, and swung. The lich exploded into dust and bone as time suddenly resumed—like someone had pressed play. Olis's robe fell into a pile, and his skull clattered to the floor. I drew in a deep breath and collapsed to my knees, suddenly feeling super tired.

16

ARMY OF THE DEAD

"No time for that!" Darius snapped.

Before I knew it, Bruno had pulled me up and placed the handle of my dagger into my palm. We burst out of the room, but I was so dizzy that I kept tripping. I dropped my daggers and Bruno snatched them up with one hand while steadying me with his other.

"Carry him!" Darius shouted, and his voice sounded faraway.

Although I knew Bruno was a baby giant, I was still surprised how easily he scooped me up and threw me over his shoulder. My eyes started to droop as I bounced along on Bruno's shoulder, and I had almost drifted off when a loud crash woke me up. The druid screamed and shoved passed Bruno as something enormous exploded through one of the castle walls. I finally knew what had made the elephant-like footprints we'd found in the courtyard.

It was probably fifteen feet tall and looked like a sumo wrestler, except it was bald, was missing its right eye, and had stitches crisscrossing its entire body. Its skin color also didn't match. While its arm was a pasty white, its hand below a line of stitches was brown. It was like that all over its disgustingly obese body, as though someone had played mix and match with old body parts.

"Flesh golem!" Darius shouted.

The creature bellowed—a sound like an elephant trumpet mixed with the roar of a lion—and ran at us. Darius turned while running and waved his hand at the monster. An explosion rocked the hallway, and fire caught hold of the nasty old rug on the floor. The flames shot up in front of the flesh golem, but the big undead monster barely flinched as it barreled through the fire. Darius tried this twice more, slowing the monster down enough for us to break right and run down the stairs.

The druid tripped and rolled down the staircase, scrambling to his feet as we reached the bottom. Darius turned to look up the stairs at the charging flesh golem. He made a sign with his right hand and the stone steps cracked and caved in on themselves. The monster bellowed in surprise and disappeared from sight as it fell through the stairs to whatever was underneath.

Feeling better, I said, "Put me down, Bruno."

Bruno set me on my feet and handed back my daggers. The green dude—again in his normal shape and wearing a hat and now broken sunglasses—gibbered something urgent at me, like he was trying to warn me. I was about to ask Darius what the green dude was freaking out about when Darius grabbed me by the arm with his free hand and pulled me into a run.

The screeching started.

"Wraiths!" Darius blurted out.

Streams of thick, black smoke streaked out from the shadows all around us and formed into human-like shapes with glowing red eyes. We'd just reached the castle's entrance when an explosion from behind us rocked the world. I glanced backward and saw the flesh golem climbing out from a gigantic hole in the bottom of the staircase.

Darius formed another ball of light in his hands and yelled, "Close your eyes!"

He lobbed the ball over his shoulder like a grenade, and I shut my eyes just as an explosion of white light lit up the whole castle. It was so bright I could see it through my eyelids. I heard the wraiths screech and the flesh golem bellow. I opened my eyes and followed Darius out of the castle.

We sprinted through the courtyard, passing the big fountain. When we reached the arched gate, another loud bellow from the flesh golem rang out behind us. The rotund creature tore one of the castle's double doors off its hinges and hurled it in our direction. It crashed into the fountain, obliterating the angel statue and causing the top tiers to fall into its dry basin.

We ran hard until we reached the slope leading out of the ravine. I scrambled up, tripping a couple times, but not stopping until I got to the top of the hill. Screeches echoed up from the ravine, along with another bellow from the flesh golem. I didn't look back, but continued to run, following Darius into the trees.

Moaning—lots of moaning—started to come from all

around us and dozens of zombies appeared from within the trees. Two shambled into our path, but Darius chopped their heads off so fast they didn't even fall to the ground until we'd already run past them. More screeching pierced the night as thick black smoke streaked over our heads.

A wraith swooped down at me, but I leapt aside and took a swipe at it with my dagger. The blade passed through without hurting it at all. Keeping pace with my running, the wraith formed a head and torso, its eyes burning red. Just as it reached for me, Darius slashed at it with Lobo's sword making it screech and disappear.

"Only magic weapons can hurt wraiths!" He shouted.

"I thought these were magic!"

Darius shook his head. "Just enchanted."

That made absolutely no sense to me, but clearly he was right as I hadn't been able to harm the attacking wraith. Another wraith dove for us, but this one Bruno batted out of the air with his silver club. It made me really miss my lightning wand.

The distant bellowing of the flesh golem grew louder as it crashed through the trees behind us. With wraiths swirling above, zombies rising out of the ground all around us, and a blubbery version of Frankenstein chasing us, I was pretty sure we were going to die. Darius must've been thinking the same thing, because he skidded to a stop, turned toward the oncoming hoard, and slammed the point of Lobo's sword into the forest floor.

"Darius, what are you doing?" I shouted.

"Quiet!" he snapped, and then closed his eyes. "Get behind me."

We all did as he ordered, Bruno having to bat away a few diving wraiths. Darius's brow furrowed and he made a sharp motion with his free hand. Fire exploded in front of us, a wall of it as tall as the trees and a hundred feet wide, blasting toward the flesh golem in a wave. The blast of heat made me wince and I covered my face with my arm. When the heat lessened I looked and found the forest in front of us engulfed in a firestorm.

The flesh golem fell to its knees grunting in pain, and dozens of shambling zombies were burned to blackened skeletons. While it didn't kill the wraiths, the light of the inferno repelled them. Darius sagged, and would've fallen to the ground if I hadn't steadied him.

"Are you ok?" I asked.

Eyes still closed, he nodded. He was breathing hard like he'd just run ten miles.

"That was incredible," I said.

"Forest fires make Smokey the Bear mad," Bruno said. "He's going to find you, Darius, and spank you with his shovel."

He had a point. Well, not about the shovel-wielding bear, but Darius's spell *had* lit the forest on fire, and it was spreading—fast.

"We need to keep running," Darius panted. He pulled Lobo's sword out of the dirt.

The wall of flames in front of us parted, and Olis floated out of the fire. The lich was whole again, as though Darius had never attacked him. Darius's face paled.

"You killed him," I said. "I saw it!"

Olis laughed. "Ignorant child! You can't kill something that's already dead!"

"RUN!" Darius lobbed a ball of light at Olis making the lich cover its glowing green eyes.

The druid and the green dude were already dashing through the trees when Bruno and I started running. I ran so fast that my P.E. teacher would've been surprised. Who's the disgrace now, Coach Thompson?!

The night lit up as a bolt of lightning struck a tree on my left. The tree creaked as the trunk splintered, and the top began to fall. It crashed down only a foot or two behind us. More bolts of lightning lit up the night as Olis's laughter echoed through the trees. He was toying with us. We really *were* nothing to him.

I ran so fast and so recklessly that I choked and nearly fell backward to the ground when Darius pulled on the back of my shirt.

"What are you...?" I cut off when I saw that the ground a few feet in front of me dropped away. We were at the edge of some kind of ridge. I couldn't see the bottom of the cliff, but it was clearly a long fall, and I could hear the faint sound of rushing water.

"There's a river down there!" I said.

Darius nodded. "I think I know which one. If I'm right, it marks the southern edge of the forest. The undead can't follow us if we make it there."

We turned around, our backs to the precipice. Olis floated down to the ground in front of us. "Looks like our little game has reached its conclusion."

"Darius, what do we do?" My voice cracked—again, from fear, not puberty.

"We need to get to the river." He held Lobo's sword out in front of him, sharp point toward Olis.

"But we don't have time to climb down!"

"No, we don't," Darius agreed. Then he shoved me with his free hand, launching me off the cliff and into the air.

Though it felt like I was falling through darkness for eternity the sound of rushing water quickly became louder and I had just enough time to suck in a short breath before I plunged into the freezing river. Blackness surrounded me and I had a hard time trying to find "up." Splashes above and to the side helped me orient myself and I began kicking as hard as I could.

I gasped when my head broke the surface. Fortunately, my short career in scouts had included swimming, and water safety, so I was able to tread water; although I couldn't stay in place because the swift current forced me downriver. I was finally able to stop myself by letting the current push me up against a rock. I looked up toward where we'd jumped. Two green glowing dots peered down at us. They were so distant that they could've been stars.

Bruno splashed and struggled to stay above water as the current carried him past me. I reached out and caught the collar of his shirt, stopping him and giving him a chance to grab onto my hand and swim over to my little rock island.

Darius and the druid climbed out of the river onto a muddy bank. The green dude had morphed into a flat circle that let him float on top of the water like algae, and so only needed to slither onto the bank where he re-took his normal form. "Normal" probably wasn't the right word, "usual" form would be more accurate. Remarkably his *disguise* of black hat and sunglasses remained in place.

Bruno and I made our way together over to the river bank where we climbed up and joined the others. I found Darius staring up at the cliff.

"He can't get us?" I asked.

"Doesn't look like it," he said.

I sighed. "Then we're finally safe."

"Safe?" Darius's tone was sharp. "Do you know where we are?"

I was surprised by Darius's sudden anger. Afraid to say anything, I just shook my head.

"Well neither do I! We're lost!"

"But you said the river..."

"This river runs for hundreds of miles, if it's even the same river!" He gripped the sides of his head with both hands. "And now we have a powerful lich for an enemy and it's all his fault!" He pointed at Bruno.

Bruno's wet hair hung down over his eyes making him look like a sheepdog.

"And you!" Darius took a step toward the druid and threw a finger at him. "You're a fool and a liar!"

The druid pointed at his chest, his eyes wide in disbelief.

"If it weren't for you and your pet blob over there, we never would've had to go chasing after Bruno!"

The green dude gibbered something that sounded angry.

"I should've left you three in Zombieville!" Darius turned back to me. "And so help me, Thomas, if they get into danger again, I won't be so charitable. I will let them die before I risk failing my quest!" Darius stormed off into the darkness.

After a long, uncomfortable silence, Bruno whispered to me, "So, is he mad?"

I looked at Bruno with wide eyes. "Are you serious?"

He shrugged. "Sorry, I wasn't really paying attention."

17

THE MOUNTAIN OF TRIAL

We didn't stay on the banks of the river, but hiked a couple miles away just to be as far from Echo Wood as we could before sleeping. Darius wouldn't talk to me, not even when I tried to ask him about what'd happened in Olis's chamber when everything but the five of us froze. We eventually found a suitable spot to camp, and when morning came I woke up to find Darius gone. At first I worried that he'd abandoned us, but just before midday, he came back into camp.

"Darius!" I stood up from the log I was sitting on.

"Hey, druid told us you were dead!" Bruno said.

Darius glowered at the druid. "You know he's a pathological liar, don't you?"

Bruno laughed. "Cool. I know a pathological liar."

"Hey!" the druid said. "Why do you assume I'm always lying? Just cuz my tales can't be backed up with evidence, logic, or common sense?"

"Where've you been?" I asked.

"I went to scout ahead, and try to figure out where we are." Darius removed his pack, and set it on the ground. He knelt in front of it and began to rummage through his things. After a moment he pulled out a rolled piece of parchment. Darius unrolled the paper and put it on the ground. It was a map.

"You see this?" Darius pointed at a squiggly line drawn in blue. It ran through a big cluster of trees, and then continued west.

"I found Waldo!" Bruno shouted and reached out to touch the map.

Darius batted his hand away. "I think this is where we are." He pointed at the line representing the river. "And this is where we need to go." He traced his finger to the south east of the map to an island in the middle of a large body of water."

"That's not too far," I said.

"It's not the distance I'm worried about," Darius said. He pointed at a large mountain nearby our current position. "To get to the island where my father hid the crystal, we're going to have to go over this mountain."

I read the scribbled note next to the picture of the mountain. "Mountain of Trial."

"It's an active volcano. And that's not the worst of it." He pointed to a yellow patch on the far side of the mountain.

"Desert of Woe," I read.

"I've heard things about that place," Darius said. "Disturbing things."

"Like more undead monsters disturbing?" the druid asked. "Or seeing grandma in the shower disturbing?"

"*Mountain of Trial? Desert of Woe?* Isn't there a shortcut through like the Canyon of Happiness or something?" Darius didn't laugh at my stupid joke. Instead he just glared at me.

"Because of what happened last night, we don't have time to backtrack to the Jora road, or escort these morons to safety."

"Pfft!" The druid scoffed. "You all are just lucky I was there to..."

I shook my head at the druid and he shut up. I didn't want him to make Darius mad again.

"They can travel with us, but they have to keep up." Darius glanced at the druid and the green dude. "I won't slow down for them, or wait for them if they fall behind."

I nodded, not wanting to argue with Lobo's son when he was like this, which I later came to realize was almost all the time. For someone so young, he sure was grumpy.

"We need to get moving, the mountain is only a half a day's hike from here." Darius rolled up the map and stowed it away in his pack.

"Half a day" might've been what it would take Darius to reach the mountain if he were alone, but for the group of us, it took almost eight hours. It was partly my fault, though. I was still tired from escaping the forest of horrible nightmares and horribleness, not to mention only getting a few hours' sleep. I think Darius realized this, because we didn't receive the usual amount of scolding, insults, or demands for more hustle. And he only threatened to kill the druid twice, which, for Darius, was downright charitable.

When we finally reached the base of the Mountain of Trial, the sun was low on the horizon. The mountain itself wasn't terribly tall, but its slope was pretty steep. Black smoke billowed out from the peak of the mountain, which was flat, confirming that the Mountain of Trial was indeed a volcano.

I sat down on a rock.

"What are you doing?" Darius demanded.

I glanced at the others and then back at Darius. "It's almost night. Aren't we going to camp?"

"Yeah!" Bruno said. "I wanna make s'mores!"

"Do you realize what you did last night?" Darius asked.

I shook my head.

"You used the Crystal of Time's power."

Thinking it through over the last day made me suspect as much. Though, I couldn't begin to tell you how I did it.

"And it saved us," I said feeling a little annoyed.

"It also sent an arcane ripple across the entire universe!" Darius sounded mad again.

"Which means what?"

"It means," Darius said through clenched teeth, "that Adrayen felt it, and will send Arvek after us now. He can't risk you learning how to use the crystal, because if you did you would have the power to challenge him."

"But Arvek was going to catch up to us anyway," I said.

"Instead of waiting until you have the crystal, Adrayen will send Arvek to intercept us, or at the very least watch us. When he sees that I'm leading you, he'll attack. That's why we can't afford to dally."

"I have a dolly," Bruno said. "His name is Arthur, and he used to be a for real, *live* kitty..."

I knew Arvek wouldn't come until I called him with Adrayen's spell. The guilt I suddenly felt drove away my irritation and made me want to throw up. "So I guess I shouldn't try to use the crystal anymore." Not that I had tried in the first place, it just happened.

"Absolutely, not! Aside from sending up a magical flare visible to the entire universe, the effort drained your strength."

I thought of how I'd nearly collapsed from weakness after time resumed.

"Frankly, you're lucky it didn't kill you! Using that much power untrained..." He didn't finish.

"I get it," I said.

Darius stared at me for a long moment before saying, "Besides, I'm not convinced we're out of Olis's reach."

"But he didn't come after us."

The druid raised his arm and flexed his bicep. "I think he got one look at this and thought better of it."

"I have a *non-delusional* theory about that." Darius drew in a deep breath. "I think the legends are true in that something did go wrong with his spell. Not only did that malfunction create the Necrotic Expanse, but I think it trapped Olis so that he couldn't leave the Expanse. Otherwise, he would've left long ago."

"But he said that was because he was building up an undead army to attack the Crossroads."

"Oh, I don't doubt that he is. But I'm sure he uses that to cover the fact that he can't cross the river or travel beyond the Expanse's borders."

"Then why are you worried?" I asked.

"Olis is a lich."

"Darius said a bad word," Bruno giggled.

"Do you understand what a lich is?"

"Yeah," I said. "He's an old, dead wizard."

"Old doesn't begin to describe him. Try ancient. With that much time on his hands to learn and practice his spells, he has become very, very powerful."

"Is that why he was able to come back after you killed him?" I asked, remembering the pile of bones lying on top of Olis's robes.

Darius sighed. "He can't be truly killed unless we destroy his phylactery."

"Olis has a factory?" Bruno said. "Like Willie Wonka?"

Darius rolled his eyes. "A phylactery is a magic item—usually a metal box—that holds the lich's soul. Unless that is destroyed, Olis will just keep coming back no matter how many times he's killed."

That made me glance back up to Echo Wood on top of the canyon wall. "He knew I held the crystal's bond."

"And he won't rest until he gets the crystal. I'm sure it would let him overpower the magic that keeps him trapped. That means he'll be sending his minions after us, or worse."

"What's worse?" I asked.

Darius shook his head. "You've made a powerful enemy, Thomas." Then he just turned away and started hiking toward the mountain.

For the first hour, the Mountain of Trial consisted mainly of a winding path that was about as steep as the stairs in my school. But just when I had begun to think the climb wouldn't be so bad, we ran into a sheer, rock wall.

"You've got to be kidding!" I complained. "We have to climb that?"

Darius smiled. "It's going to be like this all the way to the top, so don't fall behind, and don't look down." With that, he found a handhold and pulled himself up onto the wall.

This won't be so hard, I told myself. After all, our scout troop had often gone rock climbing. Except, that was always in an air conditioned building on a fake wall with brightly colored rubber handholds and safety harnesses attached to lines to catch us if we fell. And to be honest, the last time hadn't gone all that well. I still feel bad about Billy Erickson's jaw. It probably sucked not being able to open your mouth for two whole months.

I took a deep breath, and began to climb. Just when I'd gotten about fifteen feet up, I heard the green dude jabbering wildly. I looked down past the druid and Bruno who had both started climbing the wall, and saw the armless, green creature staring up from the ground. *Why didn't he just grow a tentacle?* I wondered. But for whatever reason, he was apparently unable to climb.

"Will someone just carry that thing?!" Darius shouted.

"Me, me!" Bruno called.

He climbed back down and made to put his arms around the gelatinous green creature when suddenly it changed shape, morphing so that it molded its self onto Bruno's arms and torso like a slimy T-shirt. The green dude's head encased the back of Bruno's placing the hat so that it looked like Bruno was the one wearing it, while the sunglasses rested on the back of Bruno's skull.

"Look Thomas!" Bruno laughed. "I'm wearing him!"

"Now that is just wrong!" the druid said with a shiver.

The next few hours passed in relative quiet, everyone too

busy making sure they didn't fall to their deaths for there to be any real conversation. Surprisingly, I didn't have to worry about Bruno like I thought I might. The big kid's upper body strength made lifting himself from handhold to handhold look easy. He laughed as he easily passed by me, climbing above me so I was staring up into the green dude's sunglasses for the rest of our climb.

A red glow from the top of the mountain gave us our light, and when that wasn't enough, Darius would conjure a glowing orb. By midnight, we'd reached the top of the mountain which was a bowl-shaped crater filled with bubbling, red lava. The heat hit me like a wall, and was almost painful.

"Is that strawberry jam, Thomas?" Bruno asked, licking his lips.

"Oh, absolutely," the druid said, smiling and motioning for Bruno to try some.

The green dude gibbered an answer from the back of Bruno's head, which was probably its way of telling him that the bubbling, red liquid was in fact not strawberry jam, but a molten pool of horrible death. At least that's what I imagined him saying; I guess he could've been telling dirty jokes or reciting the pledge of allegiance for all I know.

"We cross there." Darius pointed to several evenly spaced stone pillars rising ten feet out of the lava to form a crossing through the middle of the crater. Each one was flat on the top, and not much more than three feet wide.

"Why would anyone build this here?" It looked like something you'd have to jump across in the end stage of a Mario game.

"To cross the crater, of course," Darius said in a tone that made me feel like I'd asked the dumbest question in the world.

"Is this really *that* highly traveled of a path? I mean, who builds stone pillars in the bowl of a volcano. *How* does someone even *do* that?"

"Look," Darius said. "We're crossing here."

"We can't go around?" I motioned to the rocky edge that curved around the bowl of lava.

Darius shook his head. "Too slow, and too dangerous."

"And *this* is safe?" I waved at the pillars.

"Don't worry, I have a plan." Darius turned to face me, closed his eyes, and began chanting under his breath.

The druid cringed and cried out, "I knew it! He's going to turn us inside out and ride our carcasses to safety!"

"Shut up, you moron!" Darius barked. "I'm casting a spell on you that will help you maintain your balance."

"Oh," the druid said sheepishly. "I'm cool with that."

"Now keep silent so I can concentrate!"

Darius began again, and when he finished the incantation, a weird feeling came over me. It's hard to describe, but I suddenly felt like a ninja, and the idea of jumping from stone to stone across the lava wasn't as scary as it was a minute ago.

"This is awesome," I said, now feeling like I could run and clear the entire crater in one jump.

"Now this spell has a side effect," Darius warned. "Your new sense of confidence will tempt you toward..."

The druid whooped loudly as he leapt from the crater's edge onto the first stone pillar.

"...recklessness," Darius finished with a tired sigh. "Or in his case, brainlessness."

I watched as the druid jumped from pillar to pillar, laughing and sometimes stopping to dance before finally reaching the opposite side where he threw up his arms in victory and shouted, "I am the champion! The greatest hero ever! Suck on that, Darius-grumpy-pants!"

Darius waved a hand and muttered something. The druid's grin disappeared, his face turned white, and his eyes grew wide. He looked down to where he stood at the edge of the crater, shrieked, and fell backward to the ground where he pulled his legs up to his chest and began to rock back and forth. Darius flashed me a small smile and then leapt four feet from the crater's edge onto the first stone pillar. I let Bruno – still wearing the green dude like a shirt – go next before following.

I'd just landed on the second stone pillar when a vision flashed in my mind. It was of the lich, Olis. He was leaning over a bowl filled with glowing water. In the water, instead of Olis's ugly reflection, I saw me, standing on the pillar surrounded by lava. Olis was waving his bony hand over the water and chanting something. The vision ended.

"Come on, Thomas!" I heard Darius shout.

I looked up at him, and he must've seen the expression on my face, because he called, "What's wrong?"

Before I could answer, a deep rumble came from within the crater itself. A second later, a jet of lava exploded up behind me, completely enveloping the first stone platform. I covered my face with my arm to ward off the heat from the blast. The lava in the crater below me bubbled and swirled faster and faster. I looked up to see Darius urgently waving me on.

"MOVE!" he screamed.

I snapped out of my frightened stupor and leapt to the next platform just as another jet of lava shot up and enveloped the pillar behind me. "It's Olis!" I shouted.

Against Darius's warning, I tried to stop time again. It didn't work. I wasn't sure if I was doing it wrong, or if my body just didn't have the energy. Panic started to set in, and I jumped to the next platform, landing too close to the edge and pin-wheeling my arms until I caught my balance. If it hadn't been for Darius's dexterity spell, I'm sure I would've fallen into the lava.

Lava blasted up from below and swallowed the platform behind me. It was coming faster now, and I knew Olis wasn't messing around. Why was the lich trying to kill me? I thought he wanted me to bring him the crystal.

I leapt to the next pillar and hadn't even landed when the volcano swallowed the column behind me. I readied myself for another desperate jump when a jet of lava shot up in front of me, destroying the next pillar.

Ten feet now separated me from the safety of the crater's far side. "Darius!" I screamed. "I can't jump that!"

"Stay calm," Darius shouted and another rumble from below made it sound like the volcano was laughing at us. No, not the volcano, but Olis.

"What do I do?" I shouted back.

"The crystal gives you access to magic! Focus on making your legs stronger and will it to happen!"

"Are you crazy?" My voice picked that time to crack.

Just then the lava surrounding the pillar on which I stood began to roil and churn. Fear took over and I jumped, focusing on my legs as Darius had said and wishing with everything I had that they'd launch me high into the air and all the way to the crater's far side.

It didn't work.

An explosion of lava shot up just as I jumped, destroying the last platform only a heartbeat after I jumped from it. The tongue of liquid fire was so close that the heat burned my skin. But that didn't really faze me because in a few seconds I would be swimming in lava.

I fell far short of the crater's edge and plunged toward the mass of bubbling red death. No extra lives for me. No save point. No, I was going to die. I covered my face as the lava raced up to meet me. It must've been my terror that made it happen, but something clicked in my brain and I felt power flood into me, like I was being shocked, but without the pain, frozen muscles, or clenching jaw. I had only one thought in my mind at the time, and that was that I wanted to be up where Darius and the others were. I wanted it so badly, more than I'd ever wanted anything else in my life.

One second I was about to take a lava bath, and the next I was lying on volcanic rock. I raised my head and found everyone staring down at me. I pushed up to my knees and hugged myself to stop my hands from shaking.

"How?" My voice trembled.

"Teleportation," Darius said with a frown.

"Guess that was easier than turning me into Superman? Why didn't you just tell me to do that?" My sarcasm sounded forced.

Darius shook his head. "That is an incredibly advanced and complex spell. I've been training in the arcane almost my whole life, and I still can't manage it."

I shrugged, not knowing what to say to that. "Beginner's luck?"

"Nah," the druid said. "I can do it too. I just don't like to show off."

"Right," I said.

The whole mountain shook, and an angry sounding rumble came from inside the volcano.

I scrambled up. "I don't think Olis is happy we made it."

"Down the mountain!" Darius shouted. "Quick!"

Darius's magic ball of light floated after us as we climbed down. This side of the mountain wasn't so sheer, so we were able to move faster than before. And going down is always faster than going up, I guess. But that was kinda the problem. It was still a lethal drop if we lost our footing and rolled the wrong way.

We hadn't made it down very far when an explosion rocked the mountain. The entire sky lit up red as a geyser of lava shot up from the volcano's peak. I lost my hold and slid down about ten feet before I was able to stop myself by grabbing hold of a thick bush. I looked up and saw glowing red streams flowing down toward us.

"Go!" Darius shouted.

We gave up on being careful and just moved down the side of the mountain as quickly as we could, often sliding several feet at a time when we lost our holds. The rocks and bushes tore up my shirt and pants, and I had a hundred scrapes and small cuts.

Still the lava gained.

"We're not going to make it!" I shouted to Darius. "I have to use the crystal again!"

"No!" Darius snapped. "Stopping time for just a few seconds nearly killed you the last time."

"It's that or be burned alive!" I shot back. I was proud of myself for standing up to him.

I heard Bruno start to whimper. "That melty Jello is going to get us?" he asked.

"Don't worry, Bruno," the druid said in what I think was supposed to be a comforting tone. "It should only take five to ten minutes before we're burned beyond the capacity to feel pain. Then it will just be like going to sleep in a really warm blanket."

Bruno started to cry.

"Not helping!" I shouted.

"What?" The druid sounded hurt, and I think he was actually trying to help. Which, now that I think about it, is even more disturbing than him just being a jerk.

"I'm going to try something," Darius said. When I didn't reply he looked at me. "Well, don't just stay there. Move!"

We continued our reckless descent while Darius stopped and began chanting. I kept looking up at him as the lava flowed closer. When it was close enough to cast a red light on Darius, he flung out his arms and shouted something. Thunder rumbled and immediately icy rain began to pound our side of the mountain. Each drop was like a tiny, frozen slap on my face and arms, and the howling wind threatened to blow me right off the mountain. But it was working. Loud sizzle sounds came from the lava streams and white steam erupted into the air.

Lightning lit up the sky, and Darius climbed down as fast as he could. When he came to me, he said, "I've cooled the lava but it's still flowing, just slower. Hopefully that will buy us enough time to make it down the mountain."

It did, and we were able to make it to the bottom of the Mountain of Trial before the lava started flowing again. Though we were all exhausted, Darius looking the most drained, we didn't stop at the base of the mountain. No, we kept running until we reached higher ground where we were certain to be safe from the lava.

There we all collapsed; so tired that we didn't even bother to set up camp.

18
THE DESERT OF WOE

Still expecting Arvek to show up at any moment, Darius got us up after only four hours of sleep. It was late morning when we started on a path that would take us straight through the Desert of Woe. I glanced back every now and again to see smoke billowing out of the top of the Mountain of Trial, and I could see red lines running down the mountain like blood.

Darius assured me we were out of Olis's reach, but said we needed to stay alert for when he sent one of his undead minions after us. That made sense, but I wasn't too worried while we traveled in daylight, and the further we got away from Echo Wood the safer I felt. Maybe it was that or I was just distracted by the guilt that was tearing a hole in my chest.

Darius had risked his life three times now to save us, and I was still planning to betray him. I almost confessed what I'd done a couple of times, but the mental picture of Mom's grave always made me hold back. I had to get home, no matter what.

I thought a lot about what I'd done with the teleportation spell. Apparently that was a big deal. Could I manage to teleport back home? I asked Darius, making it sound like I wanted to find a magician who could do it for me.

"Personal teleportation isn't the same spell as interdimensional travel," Darius explained. "They're related, but being able to create a bridge between worlds takes far more power than even I have, and I'm considered strong among magicians."

That depressed me, and I spent most of the day keeping to myself, wishing I had my phone and music. Listening to the druid embellish tale after tale of his many supposed accomplishments just wasn't passing the time fast enough. And I was fairly certain he'd never been president of the Mole People.

By late afternoon we came upon the desert. I was surprised that it happened so abruptly. It was like we were walking on grass surrounded by trees one minute, and then about to step onto an endless ocean of sand the next. Thick green grass ran right up to the edge of the desert, making it look completely unnatural.

"It's like a great big sandbox!" Bruno clapped.

"Except you can't get lost or die in a sandbox," Darius said.

"I had an adult cousin who got lost and died in a sandbox." The druid said. "At least, that's what we assumed happened. We found him buried there, anyway. Well most of him..."

"What happened here?" I asked. "It looks like someone dropped a nuclear bomb."

Darius shook his head as he stared out over the sand dunes. "I don't know. No one does."

I shielded my eyes with a hand. "Well I can see the ocean in the distance, so the desert can't be too big."

"Are there giant worms and spice here?" The druid asked.

"Let's hope not." Darius drew in a deep breath.

"Why do they call it the Desert of Woe?" I asked. Darius not knowing what to expect made me more nervous than if he'd told me there was a giant worm hiding under the sand.

"Because very few have made it out alive, and those who have were insane, so no one really knows. But one thing is sure." Darius turned back to look at us. "This place is cursed."

"They say only music can break the desert's spell," the druid said in his silly dramatic voice.

"Who says that?" Darius demanded.

The druid looked surprised. "What?"

"Who says that only music can break the desert's spell?"

The druid glanced at me and then back again at Darius. "Um...people?"

"What people?" Darius asked mercilessly.

The druid looked even more dumbfounded. "You know: Bob...and Frank...that guy from the trailer park. Hey, I didn't expect you to call me out on this!"

"Jackass," Darius muttered. He stepped onto the sand, leaving prints behind him as he trudged up a large dune.

"Come on," I said with a sigh.

A couple of hours after we entered the desert, something weird started to happen. Bruno, the druid, and the green dude became very irritable. At first I thought it was just because we were all exhausted and the desert was hot, but as the day stretched on I realized something was really wrong. My suspicions were confirmed when the druid and the green dude got into an actual fight; just a scuffle, but it left the druid with a bloody nose.

They had argued—well, the druid argued at the green dude, who just gibbered with rising irritation—over who was more attractive: mermaids or female Sasquatch. I don't know what was more disturbing, the druid's crush on fish chicks, or the green dude apparently having a thing for Bigfoot's sister. What *would* those children look like? Eww.

Anyway, the argument turned violent when the druid said "You don't even know what you're talking about," to which the green dude jabbered something mean. Don't ask me how I knew that, I just did.

The druid shouted back, "Yeah, well so's your mama!"

I turned around just in time to see the druid fly back and land on the sand, a trickle of blood running out of his left nostril.

"You hit me!" he yelled.

Before I could do or say anything, the druid jumped to his feet and rushed forward. He tackled the green dude to the sand and began to pummel him, but the green dude turned his skin to rock just as the druid landed a blow. The druid cried out and cradled his hand, giving the green dude enough time to launch the man off of him with a quickly formed, armored tentacle. Darius intervened in time to break up the fight, but the two continued to stare each other down like boxers at the weigh-in, and the druid drew a line across his throat when he thought I wasn't looking. It would've been comical if it wasn't so contentious.

Later, when Bruno was complaining about being hungry, I joked that if we didn't stop for lunch, Bruno might just kill and eat us. I laughed, expecting Bruno to join in, but he didn't. He had a strange look on his face; a slight grin with a quick lick of the lips. If I didn't know better, I would've thought he was actually considering cannibalism.

Whatever curse was on the desert, it affected Darius too. But since he was always grumpy, I didn't notice until I asked him about the weird behavior of the others. Darius scoffed and said, "I told you they would be nothing but trouble." Then he lowered his voice and said to me, "You know, if they didn't make it out of this desert, no one would think twice about it."

I tried to laugh it off, but Darius didn't smile. I started to develop a theory for why people went missing here, and why those who *did* make it out went crazy. But why wasn't I turning creepy-crazy? Well, if I was crazy, would I even know it?

The scary behavior of the others only got worse the rest of the day, although our common goal of surviving the desert prevented any more *altercations*. By nightfall, no one was speaking to each other, not even when we had to work together to set up camp. We ate our dinner of beef jerky and hard bread in awkward silence, and every time I tried to start a conversation, nobody joined in. They just sat silently glowering at each other.

When Darius began to sharpen his sword and the druid

picked up a large stone, I said, "I think we're all a little tired, so why don't we turn in early?"

"Yes, Darius." The druid patted the rock that now rested in his lap. "Why don't you go to sleep?"

Darius smirked at the druid. "But I'm not tired."

The way he said it made my heart start to pound like I was about to get on a roller coaster or jump off the high dive.

"Maybe each of us should set up our own camps," I suggested.

Bruno licked his lips as he stared at the green dude. "Lime Jello."

I couldn't tell for sure if the green dude was falling under the spell, or if he'd just been reacting to the druid earlier. But when he formed a tentacle and turned it into a sharp spike, and mumbled something in a creepy, threatening tone, I knew he was being affected just like the others.

"You look really tired, Darius," the druid said with a dark chuckle. "Go on and lie down, drift into slumber. Me and my new friend, Head-basher," the druid stroked the large rock in his lap like it was a cat, "will take good care of you."

Darius leapt to his feet and pointed Lobo's sword at the druid. "Are you threatening me?"

The druid shot up with his rock held ready to throw. "I'm not, but Head-basher thinks your skull is full of candy, like a piñata! Let's find out, huh?!"

Bruno jumped to his feet and summoned his silver club, and the green dude turned his skin hard like armor as he made a loud angry noise.

"It's ok. I like crunchy," Bruno said with an evil grin. "It's like peanut brittle!"

Panicked, I stood and shouted, "That's enough!"

The others shut up and looked at me, their faces all showing surprise. Well except for the green dude, but that's because, well, you know.

"You're not yourselves!" I was surprised by how brave I sounded. "The desert's curse is making you crazy. You have to fight it!"

For a moment, it looked like they were listening to me. Darius lowered his sword and looked down like he was ashamed. The druid lowered his rock, Bruno's silver club disappeared, and the green dude turned soft again.

"That's better," I said with a sigh of relief. "Because of the curse, I think we should skip sleeping tonight and just get out of the desert."

No one said anything.

"Guys?" I said, starting to worry again.

Darius glanced at the others and then he smiled wickedly as he raised his sword. "Thomas first?"

The druid laughed as he brought his rock back up. Bruno licked his lips and summoned his silver club, and the green dude re-armored himself.

"Uh-oh," I said.

Then I ran.

"Get him!" Darius screamed out from behind me. "We can't let him escape!"

"Come back, dinner! I mean, Thomas!" Bruno shouted.

As I ran into the dark, my hands automatically went to the knives hanging from my belt.

No! I shook my head and forced my hands away from the handles. Darius's spell was trying to take control and help me defend myself, but I couldn't fight my friends. I glanced over my shoulder and the moonlight revealed the others running after me. But what if I didn't have a choice?

An image of a fireball flashed in my mind and so I threw myself to the right and landed behind a large rock just as one of Darius's flaming missiles streaked over me. I scrambled to my feet, slipping on the sand as I tore off in a new direction. Another fireball whizzed past, so close I could feel the heat. I ran toward a dark shape just ahead. I remembered seeing some boulders and solid sand formations big enough to give me cover and hoped that was what the dark shape was. Unfortunately, that's when I slipped, rolled my ankle, and tumbled down a steep sand dune.

When I rolled to a stop at the bottom I looked up to see Darius cresting the dune. He pointed down at me and shouted something over his shoulder. This time I let my hands go for my daggers, but froze when I realized they'd fallen out of their sheaths.

The others began to cautiously move down the dune making me think of a hunter creeping up on a deer. I tried to stand, but a sharp pain in my right ankle brought me back down to the sand. Desperate, I checked my pockets for anything that might help me. The only thing that I hadn't left back at camp was the friendship-harmonica Bruno had given me. I still had it tucked inside my pants pocket.

I was about to toss the useless thing away when I had another vision. Like the others, it was little more than a flash inside my mind, this time not of the immediate future, but of the past. As though I was watching from a distance, I saw all of us standing on the desert's edge. Darius was explaining the danger of the desert when I heard the druid say, "Only music can break the desert's spell."

The vision ended and I looked down at the harmonica in my hand. Could it be true? Could that fraud actually have been telling the truth for once? I glanced up at Darius, the druid, Bruno, and the green dude, all carefully coming down the sand dune in single file. I looked at the harmonica one more time, and realizing I had nothing to lose, I lifted the instrument to my lips and blew.

Immediately my friends-turned-attackers stopped and lowered their weapons. Darius had conjured a glowing orb and by that light I could see him frown in confusion. The effect lasted only a moment, and then the murderous look returned to his eyes.

A thrill of hope surged inside me, and I quickly began a sloppy recitation of "Mary Had a Little Lamb" – the only song I knew how to play on the harmonica. Darius and the others froze, dropped their weapons, and frantically tried to cover their ears as though the music was hurting them. Their pain made me want to stop, but something urged me on and so I kept playing.

Darius dropped to his knees, and a trickle of blood ran out of his ear. Then his light spell winked out. Bruno and the druid both fell to the sand, and the green dude compressed into a small ball and hardened himself. When they had all passed out, I stopped playing but kept the harmonica close to my lips just in case. After about a minute, Darius began to move. I sucked in a deep breath, ready to start playing again, when Darius said, "Thomas?"

He sounded really confused.

The others began to get up, and I could tell by their looking around that they also didn't know what was going on.

"Thomas, what happened?" Darius asked as he rose to all fours.

"You tried to kill me," I said, and then nodded toward Bruno. "And he wanted to eat me."

19

THE SEA OF AGES

Although Darius had used his magic to heal my ankle, it still felt a little stiff. I sat on a rock and took off my shoe to pour out the sand. Then I pulled off my sock, lifted my leg, spread my toes, and flexed my foot up and down.

"It will feel a little strange for a couple of days," Darius said as he walked up to me.

"Ok," I said before putting my sock and shoe back on. Then I took the other shoe off and poured out more sand. I'd done this twice already, but never could seem to get rid of all of it.

We'd just crossed the boundary out of the Desert of Woe and, having not slept at all last night, Darius said we could take a short rest. I looked over at Bruno. He'd drifted off and fallen onto his side on top of the green dude. A muffled mumble came from underneath Bruno, and I saw the gelatinous creature begin to squeeze out from underneath the big kid. The druid also looked to be sleeping on the ground, his hood drawn up to cover his face.

"I'm going to let them nap, but we probably shouldn't camp so close to the desert, just to be on the safe side." Darius sat on the rock next to me. After an uncomfortable moment he said, "You did good, Thomas. You saved us all."

Instead of making me feel proud, Darius's compliment made me sick. Guilt twisted in my chest, making it hard to breathe. Needing a distraction, I quickly asked, "So does that mean the Hero Blade will work for me now?"

Darius raised an eyebrow.

"I'm not asking to use it," I quickly added. "I just want to know…"

"If you're a hero?" Darius finished.

I shrugged. "I guess."

Darius stood and drew the sword. "Bravery alone does not make one a hero. Even a murderer can be brave if it's in his own self-interest."

My gut cramped. I had been brave, but was it just so I could get to the crystal? So I could give it to Arvek and go home?

"Then what makes someone a hero?"

Darius looked to the east where the sun was just starting to rise. "Sacrifice," he said quietly. "Giving up something dear to you for a greater good. Putting yourself and your desires, safety, and happiness second to someone else's."

The pressure on my chest got worse. How stupid it was to think the sword might work for me after I saved the others, even if I did put myself in danger to avoid hurting them. After all, I was going to betray Darius to Adrayen and put the entire universe in danger just so I could go home and forget all of this.

I'm doing it for Bruno too, I tried to tell myself. But it didn't help.

"Try it," Darius said. He offered the handle of the sword to me.

"How will I know if it works?"

"The blade will glow, and you'll feel the connection."

I stared at Darius, and then at the sword. The pit in my stomach got deeper, and my mouth went dry. I was worried that if the sword didn't react, Darius would know something was wrong.

"Ok," I finally said and then extended my hand.

Nothing happened.

My heart started to pound, and sweat ran down my neck. I looked at Darius, trying to hide my panic.

Darius just pulled the sword back and sighed. "I wouldn't think too much on that. You're really young and all this is new to you. Just because the sword doesn't recognize you as a hero doesn't mean that you can't become one."

Darius sheathed Lobo's sword and sat back down.

"The crystal protected me, didn't it? From the desert's curse, I mean."

Darius nodded. "Your connection to the arcane through the crystal is exceptionally powerful. I'm not even sure father was as strongly bonded as you are." Darius sounded bitter, almost jealous?

"Can you teach me a little bit about how to use magic?"

Darius didn't answer for a while. "You know that when you turn the crystal over to me, there's a good chance you'll lose your access to the arcane."

"I know," I quickly said. "That's why I want to know now. So I can understand a little bit before I lose it."

"It's a shame, really," Darius said. "You've demonstrated an unusual aptitude for using magic."

"You're talking about the teleporting thing?"

"Perhaps you have the talent, and the crystal has just accelerated your development."

"Does that mean I could still have magic after?"

"It's possible," Darius said.

Did that mean I might be able to learn how to get myself home? The little bit of hope I felt died when I thought of the scene Adrayen had shown me; an older version of myself kneeling at Mom's grave. Maybe that's how I did get home. But if what Adrayen said was true, it wouldn't be until I was old, and Mom was dead.

"There are two components to using magic," Darius's voice snapped me out of my thinking. "Your connection and your will. Connection is the simple part. Either you can touch the arcane or you can't. Simple exercises and tests developed by magicians over thousands of years can easily test that."

"But I have a connection."

"Yes," Darius said. "But whether that's natural or because of your bond, we'll have to wait and see."

"So the will part is like the training?"

"Think of it like a muscle." He tapped his bicep. "The more you lift, the stronger you can get."

"So it's just really about practice," I said, the mystical-ness of it all suddenly fading. Using magic was starting to sound a little too much like piano lessons.

Darius chuckled. "Yes. You learn to focus on the outcome you wish to achieve, which is usually done by reciting spells, and then *flex* your will to make it happen."

"So spells aren't magical?"

Darius shook his head. "Not really. They're just thought patterns and focusing techniques passed down from ancient magicians. Strictly speaking, you don't need to know a spell to use magic, but it helps."

"Can I practice something now?"

Darius sighed. "As you found out when you drew on the crystal, channeling magical energy takes a toll on the body. You can tire out, or worse. Right now would be a bad time to practice, seeing as you haven't slept all night."

"Ok." It made sense.

We talked about magic for a few more minutes and then Darius forced us all to get up and walk another five miles before we could finally sleep. We slept until early afternoon and then moved on, not camping again until almost midnight. When morning came, I got my first good look at the Sea of Ages. That made everyone excited and by the next afternoon we had reached the beach.

I laughed as Bruno tore off his shirt and ran toward the water. The druid followed, slipping out of his robe and running headlong into the waves. Why he happened to be wearing a leopard print speedo under his robe, I didn't want to know. I don't think the green dude liked the water, because he just hung back and watched, occasionally muttering something in what sounded like a tone of longing.

After ten minutes Darius shouted, "Get out of the water!"

Bruno stuck his tongue out at Darius and the druid made a rude gesture.

"Fine," Darius called. "The sea serpents can have you!"

Bruno shrieked and knocked the druid down as he scrambled to get out of the shallows. The druid came up out of the spray, choking and coughing as he charged for the shore.

"Are there really sea serpents in these waters?" I asked.

"No," Darius said with a chuckle.

I laughed at that. Darius was starting to feel less like a drill sergeant and more like an older brother. Not that I knew what that felt like exactly, but C.J. had an older brother, and when they weren't fighting, they actually had a lot of fun together.

Bruno and the druid collapsed on the beach, sucking in deep breaths. "So what now?" I asked.

Darius began walking toward the water. "We need to make it to the island as soon as we can." He pointed out over the ocean to a shape floating in the sea.

"That's it?"

Darius nodded. "Father hid the Crystal of Time in the ruins of an ancient temple built on the center of that island. I don't know exactly where *in* the temple he hid it, but you should be able to sense its hiding place."

"How are we supposed to get across the water?" I looked around. "I don't see a boat."

Darius smiled. "Watch." He walked to the edge of the water, stepping around Bruno and the druid who were only now sitting up. Darius cupped his hands around his mouth and called, "Sentinel of the Sea, we wish to purchase passage!"

For a moment, nothing happened. Then the waves calmed and a thick fog appeared, rising from the surface of the water some distance out. I walked over to stand next to Darius, a little scared as the mist flowed together and began rolling toward us.

"What's going on?"

Darius kept staring at the fog. "My father struck a bargain with a minor Dreja lord he'd defeated. He promised not to kill the creature if it would guard the island and serve as a ferryman for anyone who could pay the correct price; an amount known only to my father and I."

A long, black, boat sailed out of the mist. It was old, and looked like it had been underwater for a hundred years, and I wasn't even sure how it was staying afloat. Riding at the front of the small craft was a figure hooded and cloaked in a robe that was tattered and torn. He may have been trying to hide his monstrous face and claws, but the cloak really wasn't working for him. He had small black eyes and red skin. Black horns poked out of his head, one sticking out of the top of his hood. In place of a nose, he had only two dripping holes, and a spikey tail stuck out from beneath the back of his cloak. He wore shackles on his hands with chains that disappeared up his sleeve, and his long claws were black like his horns.

Bruno whimpered, and I didn't criticize him because the thing made me shiver too.

"And if someone doesn't know the correct price of passage?" I gulped.

"Then the boatman is free to claim that person as his victim," Darius said.

The small, black craft landed on the beach and Darius approached the Dreja. Forcing back my fear, I took a step toward the creature and froze. I pointed at the boatman's chest where a plastic badge was clipped to his cloak. It looked like an I.D. badge with a picture of the monster and everything. A name was printed below the picture.

"Norman?" I laughed. "His name is Norman?"

The boatman growled at me, but at that point I'd pretty much lost my fear of him.

"What of it?" Darius asked like it wasn't weird at all.

"Not exactly a frightening name for a monster."

"It's a very fierce name amongst the denizens of the underworld," he said, and I wasn't sure if he was being serious.

Darius dug into his pocket. He pulled out a gold coin, two silver coins, and three copper pieces. I guess the ferryman didn't take Crossroads crystal. I wonder what would happen if someone wanted to pay with a credit card?

"Norman" examined the money, nodded, and took it from Darius's outstretched palm. The Dreja waved us into the boat, and we began to board. When the druid stepped past the boatman, he held up his hand for a fist-bump, then acted offended and noticeably pouted when he didn't get one.

Bruno followed, patting Norman on the back hard enough to make him lose his balance. "Thanks, buddy!" Bruno said, and Norman growled. "Nathan!" Bruno laughed obnoxiously while shaking his head. "What a stupid name!"

The boatman growled again, but this time it sounded more sad and ashamed than angry.

After we were all sitting in the boat, it launched backward into the sea and slowly turned to face the island. Bruno suddenly went white, clapped his hand over his mouth, and then leaned over the side and threw up. The druid offered to take bets to find out how much rocking of the boat would cause Bruno to throw up a second time, but stopped when Darius threatened him.

A few minutes into our voyage I thought I saw something in the sky. It swooped like a bird, but disappeared back into the clouds before I could really get a good look at it. I told myself it was just a bird, but an uneasy knot in my stomach wouldn't let me dismiss it. I kept looking back at the sky, but never saw the thing again.

We sailed for a couple hours before finally arriving at the island's rocky shore where we had to climb out of the boat, scale a rock wall, and pull ourselves up over a cliff's ledge. When we finally made it to the top, Bruno knelt, leaned over the edge and puked again. I heard the boatman growl, and looked down to see his hood covered in chunky vomit.

"Sorry, Nathan!" Bruno called down, then wiped his mouth on the druid's robe.

"Hey!" the druid yelled.

Darius closed his eyes and shook his head before calling over the edge, "We shall return within half a day."

"He's going to wait?" I asked.

"The fare includes passage back to the mainland."

I turned away from the sea and took my first good look at the island. About a mile in, a dense jungle rose around the vine covered ruins of a large, stone tower. If not for the overgrowth, and cracks in the stone, the tower would have been awesome. Even rundown like it was, it was still pretty cool.

Darius caught me staring, and said, "Impressive, isn't it?"

I nodded.

"Wait until you see it up close." Darius patted me on the back, and then began heading toward the jungle.

After the desert, Darius was treating me different. He wasn't nice *exactly*, but he wasn't treating me like an idiot anymore. It made my stomach hurt.

"Home," I whispered to myself. I just had to get home and then I wouldn't even remember any of this.

"Come on," Darius called, and I followed, suddenly wanting to throw up too.

20

KAYLOR'S PROPHECY

"What about this one?" Bruno pointed at a four-foot plant with huge green leaves that fanned out.

"I don't know!" Darius snapped.

"What about that one?" Bruno pointed to another plant. "Is *it* poisonous?"

Darius stopped and whirled to face Bruno. "Why don't you eat it and find out?" He drew in a frustrated breath and walked ahead of us.

I pointed at Bruno. "Don't even think about it!"

Bruno laughed. "I think I know better than to eat strange things that grow in the wild, Thomas."

"Really?" I jogged to catch up to Darius.

"I don't know how you put up with him," Darius said as he batted aside a hanging vine.

I chuckled. "It doesn't bug me."

Darius looked at me with one eyebrow raised.

Just then I heard the sound of a vine whipping through the air followed by a loud *Slap!*

"Owww!" Bruno cried, a sound that was followed by angry gibbering and then the druid's mocking laughter.

"Well, Green, maybe if you had arms, you could've blocked it!" the druid taunted.

"Most of the time," I said with a shrug.

Darius shook his head. "You know, you're different from them. You seem to be able to handle yourself when there's danger."

"I just do what I gotta do to survive." It was supposed to sound casually brave, but when the word "survive" came out, my chest tightened.

"No, I'm serious," Darius said. "You have the potential to become a great hero."

"But the sword..."

"Just weighs your heart as it is, not as it might be," Darius cut in. "I've been thinking a lot about what I'm going to do when I bond the crystal."

"What do you mean?" I had to look at the ground so Darius couldn't see my face, because I'm sure I looked guilty.

"I'm going to find Drake."

"Who?"

"Another Destiny Keeper," he said. "The last Destiny Keeper," he added. "He and a small band of followers are all that's left of the organized force that fights against Adrayen." Darius looked ahead at the stone spire reaching out of the jungle's canopy. "It's been the rule for ages that the Destiny Keepers were to remain apart so that if they were defeated, the crystals wouldn't fall wholesale into the hands of their enemies. Also, it prevented the other Keepers from being tempted to take the crystals of their fellows."

"Has that ever happened?"

Darius shrugged. "Not that I am aware of, but it's sound wisdom. Joining Drake and bringing our crystals together is a desperate move, one that I wouldn't attempt save for Kaylor's Prophecy." Darius looked at me, and my confusion must've shown because he chuckled and said, "You've handled this all so well that I sometimes forget you don't know about such things.

"Kaylor was my father's predecessor. He was also from my world, and was probably the most powerful magician Talaria had seen in centuries. When it became evident that our world was Adrayen's next target, Kaylor used the Crystal of Time to look several years into the future, something that very few have had the power to do."

"What did he see?" Could this prophecy clue Darius in on the deal I'd made with Adrayen?

"At the time things were bad, but the guardians – those who fought alongside the Destiny Keepers – were still a force that Adrayen feared. Even so, it was obvious to our leaders that the tide was turning in Adrayen's favor and that we might soon be facing our defeat." Darius sighed. "That fact was confirmed by Kaylor when he foresaw the destruction of our world, and the destruction of the guardians as a large, organized army – which happened a few years later. Kaylor also saw something else. He foresaw that in our darkest hour, there would arise a hero able to challenge Adrayen and defeat him."

"So Adrayen is destined to lose?" The possibility made my guilt lessen.

Darius shook his head. "The prophecy is not a guarantee.

It simply said that this hero would have the power to defeat Adrayen, not that he unconditionally would."

"Oh." The spark of hope faded.

I turned back to check on the guys, just to...I don't know, make sure Bruno hadn't tried to eat the green dude or the druid hadn't sold them both into slavery for a handful of spare change or something. The druid was tapping Bruno on the shoulder, and then blaming it on the greed dude, which was making Bruno flustered, but they were still following along.

"Kaylor also prophesied that this hero would unite all of the galaxy in the battle against Adrayen, and only that hero would know how to win the day. That's why I'm willing to risk bringing the crystals together."

"So you believe that this is the darkest hour?" I asked.

Darius nodded.

"And you believe that you're the hero of Kaylor's prophecy?"

Darius frowned, hesitating before finally answering, "It would make sense that the hero would come from the same world as Kaylor himself. So, yes, I believe I can defeat Adrayen. But I can't do it alone. I'll need to unite with Drake, and recruit new guardians." Darius paused again before carefully saying, "I was hoping that *you* would join our fight."

"Me?" I laughed, pulled a drooping vine away from my face, and then glanced at Darius. He was staring at me, not even the hint of a smile on his stern face. "Wait, you're serious!"

"Completely."

"But I'm only twelve! I mean, sure I'm tall for my age,

and apparently naturally awesome with magic, and of course I'm good looking like a hero should be but..."

"I was younger than that when I started *my* training. And I'm only a few years older than you are now."

Bitter, gut wrenching guilt killed my attempts at humor and I blurted, "I'm not a hero!" It came out sounding like a confession, which I guess in some ways it was.

I jumped when Darius grabbed my arm. He stopped walking and looked me straight in the eyes. "But you could be."

I couldn't hold his gaze and had to look away.

Darius let go of my bicep. "You have courage and have demonstrated that you can fight when you have to. Perhaps that's why father chose you to hold the crystal's bond until I could find you." Darius resumed walking. "Truth be told; anyone can become a hero if they *choose* to be. Even those misfits." He threw a wave behind us.

Just then Bruno bellowed in rage, and I heard the druid yelp, "Bruno bit me!" That was followed by the sound of the green dude jabbering something that had the distinct ring of "that's what you get."

"Well, maybe not *anyone*." Darius sighed. "But Thomas, I know *you* could be a hero."

"How can you *know* that?" I scoffed.

"You have the seeds of greatness in you. That's not an assumption, or cliché saying to try to rally your courage. It's a fact. You come from noble stock."

"I don't understand."

Darius wrinkled his brow and hesitated before finally

saying, "You're just going to have to trust that I know what I'm about in this."

"Darius, I don't want to join an army and fight evil! I just want to go home!"

"I sympathize, I really do. But finding a way back to your world could take years, if you find one at all."

"So I've heard," I muttered.

"When we defeat Adrayen, we can use the Crystal of Space to send you back to Earth. It still may delay your homecoming by years, but it would be a sure thing." Darius hesitated again before saying, "I'm beginning to believe that your coming here was not an accident. I think it might be your destiny to stand with me against Adrayen and his four Dreja lords."

"I'll think about it," I said, and the lie stabbed my chest.

"That's all I ask."

After another hour of hiking through the jungle, we finally reached the ruins of what must have once been a village. In the center of a ring of crumbling stone structures rose a huge, rectangular building with a stone spire rising out of its top. Darius jogged toward the temple, Lobo's Hero Blade flashing into his right hand. Once he reached a vine covered wall, he began to hack and clear away the growth.

"Help me!" Darius barked.

I drew my knives, ran up to the wall and began cutting at the vines. Twenty minutes later the wall was cleared and two large, stone double doors stood before us. They were intricately carved with patterns and designs. I ran my hand along the face of the doors, pressing my fingers into the grooves of the runes and designs.

"How do we open it?"

Darius stepped back, extended his left hand and opened his palm. He whispered something, and I gasped as the designs on the temple doors started glowing. Green light flowed through the circular carvings like water, until all the runes and designs were lit up. A moment later, rumbling, followed by a loud scraping noise accompanied the moving doors as they slowly swung inward. It was like they were inviting us in.

"Oh sweet!" Bruno said.

"It reminds me of the Mystical Tower of Faelyon," the druid spoke in his melodramatic tone. "Save those doors were twice as large, and made of gold."

"Really?" Bruno asked, sounding impressed.

"Oh yes," the druid said. "I used to address my subjects from atop the..."

Darius glared at him and the druid's shoulders slumped.

"Fine," he said. "I used to panhandle outside the front gates, hoping to score enough coin for a kitten tattoo. Happy?"

"Come on." Darius motioned for us to follow.

"Um," the druid said. "I think we'll just stay right here, ya know, to guard the entrance. I know some intergalactic gang signs that will scare away even the most bloodthirsty foes—minotaurs, unicorns, weresheep."

"Well, I can't say I'm surprised," Darius scoffed.

"That sounds like a good idea," I quickly added. Truthfully I just didn't want the others to get hurt, or see what I was about to do.

"Thomas?" Bruno asked, his tone worried.

I patted the big kid on the shoulder. "Don't worry. We shouldn't take long."

Bruno bit his lip and nodded.

"Come on," Darius said, and we walked through the open doors.

"Can I see your kitty tattoo?" I heard Bruno ask the druid.

21

THE STONE SENTINEL

The gigantic stone doors swung closed behind us; a wave of Darius's hand causing them to stop moving just before they completely shut. That left a six inch opening between the doors' seam through which light spilled in from the outside. It was still too dark though, and I was glad when Darius started motioning with his hand to cast a spell. At first I thought he was just going to make another ball of light, but instead the spell lit up a series of small orbs mounted on the walls and hanging from the vaulted ceiling.

I chuckled. "Magic light bulbs."

Darius frowned and said, "This place is very old. Old enough that there are etchings on the walls that depict the time when the first four Destiny Keepers were entrusted with the power of the gods."

I took a step toward the stone wall and stared at the pictures carved into it. They weren't like caveman paintings, these actually looked like they'd been made by someone with skill. They showed what looked like a sunset over a gate. Four figures—two men, and two women—stood with arms raised toward the sun as four crystal shards floated down toward them.

"Those are the first four Destiny Keepers?" I pointed at the figures.

I didn't hear Darius's answer because of a sudden, powerful pull on my mind. That's the only way I can really describe it. It was overwhelming, and I could feel the Crystal of Time calling out to me. I collapsed to my knees, grabbing both sides of my head.

Then it was over and Darius was helping me stand. "Are you ok, Thomas?"

"Two floors down, in a hidden room in the basement," I blurted out.

"What?"

"The crystal," I said as I rubbed my eyes. "I know where it is."

Darius slowly nodded. "Your bond with the crystal is growing stronger."

"What does that mean?" I asked.

"It means we need to hurry."

I followed Darius across the floor of the humongous chamber. We had to walk around dozens of stone pillars that went all the way up to the ceiling. Darius was making for a wide staircase at the far end of the chamber. It led up to a split level that reminded me of an indoor running track.

As we neared the center of the room, I saw a small stone figure standing inside a circle of runes. It was rectangular, with arms and legs, and a ruby set in the top of its face that made it look like a little, blocky cyclops.

"What's that?" I pointed at the stone man.

"Nothing we need to worry about," Darius said, and he walked past it. But when I went to pass, the little statue raised its right arm as if to halt me. Darius looked back. "That's odd."

"It's not supposed to do that?"

Darius motioned to me to continue forward, and I did, walking around the little stone man's circle of runes. Just as I stepped beyond the circle the runes lit up, and a column of light shot up into the air completely swallowing the small stone man.

Darius grabbed me from behind and started pulling me away from the column of light.

"What's wrong?" I shouted.

Darius shoved me toward one of the room's stone pillars, and shouted, "Get cover!"

I opened my mouth to ask again, but froze. The column of light was gone, and the little stone man had been replaced by a gigantic creature. It looked exactly like the little stone man, except bigger, much bigger and holding a very large, very wicked stone mace. The blocky titan turned to look in my direction, its ruby eye glowing an angry red as it fixed on me.

I turned and ran for the nearest pillar, ducking behind it in a really sorry attempt to hide. I felt as much as heard the stone titan walking toward me. It stopped moving, and I saw the glare of its glowing ruby eye reflected on the marble floor. A fire ball crackled past me and struck the titan, but nothing happened. Darius shot lightning next, but again the huge stone guard was unaffected.

An image flashed in my mind, showing me the stone column I was hiding behind explode into a dozen large chunks. I jumped out from behind the pillar just as the titan swung its mace into it. Just like what I'd seen in the vision, the column exploded into a storm of dust and debris.

"What's going on in there?" The druid's voice echoed from the temple's front doors.

I scrambled for cover behind another pillar while the cloud of dust still hung in the air.

"Come and get me!" Darius shouted at the titan, the taunt followed by another flash of light and a thunderclap. For a moment, I thought the titan *had* started chasing Darius, but I was wrong. The ground shook as it got closer.

"Bruno wants to know if you guys need help," the druid called. Then I heard him gasp and I knew he'd seen the titan. "Um, they got this. Now let's go sit over there, away from the door, and not talk."

"It's only targeting you, Thomas!" Darius shouted.

"Ya think?!"

"Its weak spot is the jewel-eye! I'm going to try to circle around and hit it with a spell, but if you get the opportunity, try to strike it with your daggers."

Another warning vision flashed in my mind and I threw myself away from the pillar just in time to avoid a subsequent exploding stone column. As I scrambled away, I slipped on the smooth floor and fell to the ground. I rolled onto my back, my hands automatically drawing my enchanted daggers and twirling them into my palms. The glow from the titan's eye tinged the cloud of stone dust an evil red. I jumped up, took aim with the dagger in my right hand, and hurled it with every ounce of strength I had. The dagger spun handle over blade and sailed past the titan by a good six feet.

"Your enchantment sucks, Darius!" I shouted, feeling embarrassed.

"It must be fading!"

That the spell on my daggers had an expiration date is something I really wished he would've told me earlier.

I exploded into a run toward the far end of the chamber; the titan's thundering steps shaking the ground behind me. Had it not been for the forest of marble pillars crowding the chamber, the stone brute would've easily caught up to me. I tried to take full advantage of this, but every time I swerved to put a pillar between me and the titan, it would just pause long enough to bash the pillar to pieces with its mace before stomping on.

I reached the wide stone staircase and dashed up the stairs two at a time until I reached the split level second floor —which was more of a wide balcony that ran along the inside wall of the chamber. Several sections of the floor had huge gaps where the titan had destroyed the support pillars beneath.

"Thomas!" Darius's warning shout made me look back down the stairs to where the titan stood.

It raised its mace and brought it down on the center of the staircase, smashing the steps beneath into broken chunks of rock. I coughed as I ran along the wall, not really knowing where I was going. Everything shook and the titan bashed away the balcony behind me. I ran faster, but the titan easily kept pace. A warning vision made me stop running, and the titan's huge fist slammed into the wall right in front of me.

I fell backward to the balcony floor and rolled. A swing of the titan's mace took out the floor in front of me. I panicked as I realized the floor in front and behind was now gone, and that I stood on a section of balcony supported by just one pillar beneath. I was trapped.

I backed up against the wall and stared into the titan's one glowing red eye. It might've been my imagination, but the titan looked like it was gloating, like it knew it had me and was singing "nah nah nah nah nah." Well, it'd probably be saying something scarier than that.

I grabbed my remaining dagger and cocked back for a throw. A lightning bolt struck the titan from the side, and although the spell left a crack in its left shoulder, the stone creature didn't appear to notice or care.

"Thomas!" Darius called, his tone panicked. The thought of his trying to save me, even though it would be easier for him to just let me die made me sick.

I let the magic of the dagger take over and I hurled it at the titan's jewel-eye. It hit it, but just clattered to the floor leaving no damage. Everything went quiet as the titan and I just stared at each other. If I wasn't fighting for my life, it would've been awkward. You know, like a long elevator ride with strangers after you...um, never mind.

The titan raised its mace high in the air, and so I did the first thing that popped into my mind. I jumped onto the titan, landing on the stone creature, my hands gripping the top of its blocky head so I hung over its face.

"Thomas!" Darius screamed.

The titan rocked back and forth, trying to throw me off its face, but I just held on. Finally, it raised its huge stone fist to smash me. I let go just as it swung at its own face, hit the ground, rolled and then looked up.

The titan stood frozen with its own fist buried into its eye. A heartbeat later something clanked to the ground beside me —red shards. I looked up again and watched as the titan started to teeter backward. It wobbled for a moment, and then fell onto its back, breaking into pieces when it hit the floor.

"Thomas!" Darius ran up to me. "Are you injured?"

I shook my head, still not quite believing what I'd just done. It had been crazy and desperate and kinda funny. Not a *yo-mamma-joke* funny, but more like a *I fell off the roof but landed on a pile of garbage and didn't die* kinda funny. Ok, so it wasn't really so much funny as it was terrifying.

"What was that about?"

Darius looked at the broken pieces of the titan. "That's a stone sentinel. The spell upon it instructed it to protect this room from intruders. My father placed it here."

I stood and found my daggers. "You didn't think it would attack?"

Darius stared at me. "The enchantment instructs it only to attack allies of Adrayen."

Cold, sick, panic slugged me in the gut. "Did something go wrong with the spell?" I asked, trying to sound innocent.

"It's rare, but it does happen. Like I said, father was no magician, so he would've had someone else craft the enchantment." Darius shook his head. "It could be that whoever cast the spell was a traitor, and laid this as a trap."

Traitor? *I* was the traitor.

I was relieved when the druid interrupted us. "Do you guys need help fighting that big stone monster?" He called.

"You know perfectly well that the battle is over," Darius shouted back.

"It is?" the druid yelled, his tone obnoxiously false. "Huh."

Darius rolled his eyes. "Let's go."

22

A MOMENT IN TIME

Darius's ball of light bobbed along with us as we made our way down a spiral staircase. I flinched at every noise, expecting another of Lobo's traps or guards to try to stop us, but nothing like that happened.

At the bottom of the staircase was a big metal door with carvings on it.

"The catacombs," Darius said as he read the writing scrawled on the large door. He pressed a hand against it, whispered a spell, and it opened on a long dark tunnel.

We stepped in and when Darius's light spell floated through the door, it illuminated a long corridor lined on both sides with open doors. I looked into one of the rooms and gasped at the shelves filled with cobweb-covered skeletons.

"This is a tomb?"

"Probably for the people who once worshipped here."

I looked away from the bones. It all reminded me of our time in Olis's castle, and I didn't really wanna think about that much. "They're not going to come to life and attack us are they?"

Darius laughed. "This is sacred ground. The opposite of the Necrotic Expanse. We don't need to worry about undead here." He stopped walking and looked at me. "Can you feel where the crystal is?"

I paused for a moment, lightly touching my mental link to the crystal. "It's towards the back." I pointed, and then broke into a jog. I was so sure where the crystal was calling from, that I could've found it in the dark, even without Darius's light spell.

At the end of the long corridor, there was an open room with a large stone block in the center. There were no shelves holding skeletons here, just the rectangular stone that looked like a coffin.

"It's in here." I knocked on the lid of the stone box.

Darius nodded, and we went to work sliding the heavy stone lid over just enough to see inside. The coffin didn't have a skeleton as I'd expected, just some leather bound books, trinkets, and a small object wrapped in a linen rag. I leaned in and grabbed the bundled object and unwrapped a palm-sized crystal shard. It glowed with a blue light brighter than Darius's light spell.

"It's pretty," I said. And for some reason I felt like I had to whisper.

"Father's legacy."

I looked up at Darius and saw a tear roll down his cheek, which was weird because I'd never seen him cry.

"Although I stand to inherit one of the greatest treasures in the universe," Darius said, "I would trade it all just to have the chance to see him one more time, and say goodbye."

I saw Lobo's face. It wasn't a vision from the crystal, but a memory frozen forever in my mind; when he jumped in front of Ajii's spell, looked me in the eyes, and then turned to stone. What would he think of me now?

"When was the last time you saw him?" I asked, trying to keep my voice steady.

Darius stared at the crystal, soft light glowing blue on his face. "It was actually a couple years ago, just before I completed my mage training. I didn't realize it at the time, but when he left, he was saying more than just a normal goodbye." Darius shook his head. "He embraced me, and told me that he was proud of who I had become. He told me that I would one day save the universe from Adrayen. I thought," Darius's voice caught, "he was being sentimental because I was near the end of my training. Now I understand that he knew he was going to his death."

"You think he knew?"

"He'd used the power of the crystal to look into the future. He wouldn't tell me what he saw, but whatever it was, it filled him with a sense of urgency, and it was the reason he left."

Had Lobo seen this moment? If so, why would he trust me with the Crystal of Time? Could the future be changed? Was he trying to make me change my mind? It was all very confusing.

"Lobo was strong enough to see into the future?"

"Like with normal magic, using the crystal relies on the strength of the Destiny Keeper's will, and so it is the strength of the will that matters. And Father had an unusually strong will, like Kaylor."

"Oh," I said. It was dumb, but I wasn't sure how else to respond.

"Will is power, Thomas," Darius continued. "The stronger a person's will, the more power that person has to control their destiny or change the world. The more power they have to make things happen. It's why it's such a key component to casting spells."

I nodded, looking at the glowing crystal in my hand.

"It's time to pass the bond," Darius said.

I closed my hand around the crystal. "Not down here," I blurted out.

"What?" Darius asked. "Why?"

I thought fast for an excuse. "After what happened with Olis, being around skeletons is freaking me out." I waved my free hand at the long corridor and it's dozens of tombs. "Can we do it upstairs?"

"I told you this place was hallowed," Darius said.

"Please," I said, trying to make my voice sound scared, not that I really had to try.

Darius's brow wrinkled. "I guess."

"Thanks," I said and then turned to jog back down the corridor. I made sure to stay ahead of Darius, so he couldn't talk to me.

When we reached the top of the spiral staircase, Darius caught up with me and grabbed my arm.

"Ok, we're away from the dead now," he said.

I looked at Darius, and my insides twisted. This man— not much older than myself—trusted me. He'd even risked his life to save mine. He might even be the hero foreseen in Kaylor's prophecy. My internal conflict must've shown on my face because Darius frowned and his eyebrows raised. I could see his worry.

"What is it, Thomas? What's wrong?"

I couldn't do it while looking at Darius, so like a coward I closed my eyes.

"Thomas?"

"Sala trose, vorsik Adrayen," I blurted out, and then turned and ran out of the stairwell.

I exploded into the temple's main chamber, and froze when I saw a tall figure waiting at the bottom of the half-smashed staircase. He had a pale face, long black hair and a black leather coat that fastened across his chest. He was wearing leather gloves and a thin sword hung in a sheath at his hip.

Arvek.

Standing with him were over a dozen hunched and misshapen figures dressed in black with hoods and masks covering their faces.

Arvek flashed his vampire teeth in a smile and slow-clapped with gloved hands. "Well done, Thomas."

Darius rushed out of the stairwell. "Thomas, watch out!" He shouted, and a fireball streaked past me and down toward Arvek. The Dreja lord looked completely unconcerned and simply raised his hand, palm facing out, and caught the fireball. He closed his hand around it, snuffing it out as he squeezed.

"You should know better than that, Darius," Arvek scolded. "Your spells are useless against me."

The Hero Blade flashed into Darius's hand as he charged down the stairs. When he got to the bottom, two of Arvek's hooded creatures attacked him, and Darius managed to lop the head off of one. It fell to the stairs and rolled free of its black mask. I gasped when I saw the creature for what it really was; a grotesque human-like face with discolored skin, bulging green eyes, a horned brow, and razor-sharp teeth.

Darius shouted angrily as he was overpowered and disarmed by four of Arvek's monsters. They bent his arms behind him and forced Darius to his knees.

"Run, Thomas!" he shouted.

Arvek laughed. "You still don't see it?" He motioned at the fallen form of the stone titan.

Darius shot a look at the titan and then up at me. Our eyes met and he paled.

"Thomas, no..." he whispered.

"I'm sorry," was all I could say before looking away.

Arvek stepped right up to Darius. "You're a fool, Darius. Did you honestly think that I didn't know it was you that had hired on as my guide?"

"Then why..."

"Oh, don't get me wrong." Arvek pulled the black leather glove off of his right hand. "It wasn't part of the original plan. However, I allowed you to pull it off because I knew that you'd be the best person to help this Earth-child find your father's crystal. Was I wrong?"

Darius bowed his head in defeat.

"You're too trusting, Darius. It's a flaw that your kind shares." Arvek leaned down to look Darius in the face. "And now to make sure you don't try anything desperate."

Arvek extended his right hand to touch Darius's forehead with the black nail of his index finger. Darius struggled but the monsters in black held him down.

"Don't hurt him!" I shouted.

Arvek pressed his nail into Darius forehead and he began to scream.

"Arvek, please stop!"

Arvek ignored me. The Dreja lord's eyes were closed and a lopsided grin on his face made it look like he was enjoying himself. A moment later, he drew back his hand, sucking in a deep, satisfied breath. Darius fell forward; the hooded creatures letting him fall on his face.

"Darius!" I shouted.

Arvek looked up at me and sneered. "He's not dead."

"What did you do to him?"

Arvek flashed his vampire teeth again. "I have the rare ability to absorb magical vitality. It's a form of vampirism. I took his remaining energy and used it to strengthen myself." He chuckled. "It will be days before he has the power to conjure so much as a light spell." Arvek straightened. "Now, it is time for you to come with me."

"You'll leave Darius here? And you won't hurt the others?"

Arvek arched an eyebrow. "What does it matter? You're not going to remember any of this anyway."

"Please," I begged.

Arvek looked down at the unconscious Darius. "I'm not going to kill him, if that's what you're worried about. I am going bring him along for my master. The son of a Destiny Keeper will make a most pleasing gift for him."

"No!" I was surprised by the force of my tone.

For the first time since meeting Arvek, I saw a flash of anger in the Dreja lord's eyes.

"We had a deal, boy," Arvek growled. "The crystal for passage home and a memory wipe—nothing more."

Although I was terrified, I stood my ground. "I don't want him hurt!"

Arvek rolled his eyes. "Fine. I'll leave him here." He extended his hand. "Now come down here and let us be going."

"How do I know you won't hurt Darius?" I demanded.

Arvek frowned. "Do you really wish to return home?" He drew a glowing blue line in the air and another window in space opened up. Through it, I saw my house like I was standing across the street from it.

"Yes," I said.

Arvek smiled.

I started walking down the broken staircase, but stopped when I got a better look at Darius lying on the ground.

Darius, the man who'd rescued me when the druid was leading me to certain death. Darius, the man who had saved my life time and time again. Darius, the man who'd trusted me, even tried to recruit me to fight Adrayen.

Darius the hero.

I looked at the window in space, and through it at my house. Yellow ribbons were wrapped around my front yard's fence and the handrails leading up to my porch. I knew those ribbons were to remind everyone who saw them that I was missing. I thought of Mom, and what she must be going through. She'd lost her husband twelve years ago with no explanation, and now her son. She was alone.

It will all be wiped away, I told myself. *I won't remember anything.* The thought didn't help. It had been a lot easier to ignore the threat of Adrayen's evil when it was just a story. My friendship with Darius had put a face on those who fought against that threat, and Darius's defeat had made Adrayen's evil real. I looked at Darius, and then back at the portal to earth.

"What are you waiting for?" Arvek snapped.

I drew in a deep breath and then met Arvek's eyes. "No," I said and then slid the crystal into my pocket. "I won't go with you and I won't give the crystal to your master."

Arvek shook his head and with a wave of his hand closed the portal to Earth. "You are a stupid boy," he said as he drew his saber.

I drew my daggers—though they were no longer magical —and shouted. "Stay back!"

Arvek smirked. "Oh, don't worry, Thomas. I'm not going to kill you either." He climbed two stairs and then glanced back at his gang of hooded monsters. "Did Darius ever tell you where the Dreja come from?"

I shook my head as I backed up the cracked and broken stairs.

Arvek grinned and I could see that not just his canines were pointy, but all of his teeth were. "No one is born a Dreja. A person has to undergo a very lengthy, very painful series of enchantments in order to gain their unnatural powers. Unfortunately, the process often distorts their physical appearance and drives them mad, which is why most don't volunteer for the change."

Arvek's last words, *most don't volunteer for the change,* suddenly made sense and I shot a panicked look at Arvek's band of hooded monsters.

"Yes," Arvek said. "They were once people; enemies of Adrayen, in fact. They were guardians who we captured and then forced to undergo the Dreja transformation ritual. The side effect of insanity makes them easy to control. Now, they serve my master instead of fight him, as you soon will."

"No," I said, and my voice cracked.

Stupid puberty.

"One way or the other, you will surrender the crystal to my master." Arvek climbed another step.

Panic paralyzed me. I couldn't think, and I couldn't move. I looked to Darius and he slowly turned his head so that our eyes met. He must've read my mind, because he nodded at me. I looked at Arvek and smiled. His eyes widened in anger or fear, I'm not sure which. But it was clear he'd sensed something was about to happen because he surged forward.

I reached through the crystal with all my will and stopped time.

Arvek and his Dreja mutants froze. Darius leapt up, the Hero Blade appearing in a flash. He made for the stairs. I held onto the universe with all my strength, but my grip was slipping, and there was something different this time. Another force pushed against me. It hadn't been there when we fought Olis, but it was there now, heavy and forceful. It pressed harder until I lost my grip on the crystal's power and let go.

Time resumed and I collapsed.

When I opened my eyes I saw Darius dueling with Arvek; their moves quick and fast as they struck and parried in a blur. I'd lost my hold on time too soon, and Darius hadn't been able to strike Arvek down as I'd hoped. Now Darius had to fight the Dreja lord. Could he win? I slowly sat up, head spinning, and every part of me feeling numb.

Darius and Arvek clashed, and they strained as they tried to overpower one another.

"RUN, THOMAS!" Darius screamed.

"Darius..."

"Go!" He shouted just as Arvek broke away. "Hide!"

I was able to stand, but my legs were super wobbly. I took two steps down the stairs and then tumbled the rest of the way, passing Darius and Arvek as they dueled.

"Don't let him escape!" Arvek ordered, and his monsters all turned toward me.

I tried to stand, but I was still weak from using the crystal and was only able to stumble a few feet away from the bottom of the staircase. Arvek's brutes formed a circle around me, each snarling and waving swords, knives, or maces. I tried to run, but was backhanded by one of the mutants. Its spikey knuckles cut my cheek and the next thing I knew, I was on the ground lying in my own blood, staring at booted feet.

My mind was still sluggish like I was half asleep, and I had to struggle to form thoughts. There had to be a way out of this. Could I use teleportation again? I tried flexing my will but it hurt, like I was trying to walk on a sprained ankle. *I don't deserve to escape*, I thought. *Not after what I've done.*

"DIE BAD MONSTERS! DIE!"

I looked up just in time to see one of Arvek's mutated Dreja fly out of the circle surrounding me. The other creatures turned just as a silver club knocked aside another mutant.

"Bruno!"

The big kid thumped another Dreja thug out of the way and then reached down and helped me stand.

"Hi Thomas!" Bruno grinned.

I grinned back, having never been so happy to see him.

I heard the unmistakable sound of the green dude gibbering loudly, like it was yelling an incoherent battle cry. I looked to my right and found the druid attacking one of Arvek's brutes. He was completely covered in the green dude like Bruno had been when we climbed the Mountain of Trial, except this time the gelatinous creature formed a hard shell over the druid's chest, like a breastplate. It had also molded itself over the top of the druid's head like a helmet, leaving only the man's mouth and nose exposed. The druid's arms and hands were completely swallowed in translucent green gel, forming two whip-like tentacles at the end of each of his hands which he used to strike at the Dreja mutants and throw them out of his way. In any other circumstance, it probably would've been the most disturbing thing I'd ever seen.

"He's all warm and clammy!" the druid complained. "So very very gross." He visibly shuddered. "I think I'm gonna puke," the druid bent and dry heaved a couple times.

Before I could say anything, a tentacle whipped up and put one of my daggers into my hand. I gripped it and smiled. At the moment when all seemed lost, my friends—and I didn't have a problem calling the green dude or druid that anymore—had come to save me.

Arvek's Dreja brutes quickly regrouped and formed up another circle around us. With a shout we all rushed forward. Some of the dagger's enchantment must've still remained because I was able to score a couple of hits on the Dreja mutants, stabbing one in the stomach, and slashing another across the face. Bruno swung his massive silver club, tossing one of the monsters into the air. The druid-green-dude-combo whirled into the mutants like an insane octopus, green tentacles whipping and turning solid whenever they struck an enemy.

The battle continued like that; me and my three friends beating back the mutants and even dropping a few of them. It was going so well that I actually began to hope we'd survive this. But then a horrifying glimpse of the future flashed in my mind.

I turned in time to see the vision play out for real. It was like time stopped. Not really stopped, like when I used the crystal, but everything seemed to slow down. I knew I was yelling but for some reason I didn't hear anything. I just remember my insides freezing as Arvek rammed his black saber through Darius's stomach.

Darius's eyes widened and his mouth fell open as he looked down at the black blade plunged into his gut. Arvek grinned and slowly slid the saber out of Darius who then waivered on his feet before dropping Lobo's Hero Blade. Arvek looked him up and down and then casually shoved Darius in the chest so he fell with his back against the stairs.

The Dreja lord kicked the Hero Blade aside and raised his saber to finish Darius.

Before I knew it I had thrown one of my daggers. To my astonishment, it sank into Arvek's side. The Dreja lord jerked and cried out. He lowered his saber and with his free hand yanked the knife out of his ribs. The little thrill of hope I'd gotten from scoring a hit evaporated when Arvek glared at me, bared his fangs, and started stepping down the stairs.

"Oh crumpet," I said.

"Run Thomas!" Darius cried out.

I spun and sprinted toward the temple's open doors.

23

SEEDS OF GREATNESS

The temple doors had been forced all the way open, likely by Bruno, allowing me to run out of the temple without having to slow down. I burst out of the structure and into the surrounding jungle.

A vision flashed across my mind a heartbeat before something huge crashed through the trees and landed in front of me. The impact shook the ground and I tripped and stumbled to one knee. A gigantic, skeletal claw raked the ground in front of me. I gulped. Looking up, I saw what I can only describe as a zombie dragon. It was mostly bones, but had just enough skin on its wings to allow it to fly. A ball of green energy glowed inside its massive rib-cage and its eyes burned red. I finally figured out what that big flying thing in the sky had been, you know the one I'd seen on our boat ride to the island? Apparently Olis hadn't given up on killing me. You have to admire the guy's determination.

"Crumpet, Crumpet, CRUMPET!" I scrambled to my feet.

The zombie dragon roared. I'm not sure how it did that without lungs, but whatever.

"What is the meaning of this?!"

I glanced behind me to find Arvek looking up at the monster.

"You dare interfere with the work of my master?"

The dragon lashed its bone tail, splitting a tree in half.

"Withdraw your pet, Olis!" Arvek demanded.

The dragon reared back and opened its skeletal maw. I scrambled up and threw myself to the right, tripping, but staying on my feet and exploding into a run. My back burned as a blast of heat erupted behind me. I was so scared that I didn't even glance back, but I could smell the smoke and hear the crackling of flames. Apparently dead dragons could still breathe fire—neat.

For a second I hoped that the zombie dragon had killed Arvek, but that hope died when I heard the Dreja lord shouting. What did it say for my chances of survival if Arvek could survive being blasted by dragon fire?

I ran through the vines and waist-high brush, wincing each time I was cut or scraped by branches and thorns. I finally worked up the courage to glance back. The red glow of fire outlined the top of the jungle canopy, and lots of crashing around accompanied the fall of several trees. Arvek was fighting Olis's zombie dragon.

I turned to look ahead just in time to put on the breaks and barely avoid plummeting head first over a sudden drop in the ground. I grabbed a young tree and teetered on the edge of a gully with what was easily a fifty-foot drop before regaining my balance. On the opposite ridge was a small waterfall spilling over a rocky cliff and pooling into a pond in the center of the gully below.

I looked in the direction of the temple and saw the dragon's tail whip up above the tree line. More fire was spreading from tree to tree. I had to hide, and a place with water sounded like a great idea at the moment. I found vines tethered to an overhanging tree branch above me and grabbed onto the thickest one, wrapping it around my hand like a rope. Then I backed up five feet, towing the vine with me, took a deep breath, and launched into a run. My feet left the edge of the gully and I swung out over the pond. The thought that in a different situation, this might've been fun occurred to me, bringing back flashes of summers spent camping with Mom and my relatives. But an undead dragon and a magic vampire hadn't been trying to get me back then.

When I was over the darkest part of the water, I let go of the vine and fell dozens of feet, splashing down into the pool. My butt bounced off the pond's rocky floor, and I realized just how shallow the water really was. If I hadn't landed exactly where I did, I very well could've killed myself.

I surfaced, and swam toward the shore. Soon my feet touched the ground and I was able to wade the rest of the way out of the water. I dropped to my knees on the muddy bank, looking for a place to hide. There was a large hole in the rock wall of the gully, covered by vines. I wasn't exactly thrilled with the idea of forcing my way in there with the bugs and possibly worse things, but it beat the alternative.

Something splashed into the water behind me and I glanced over my shoulder.

Arvek stood in the shallows holding the cracked skull of

the zombie dragon in his left hand and his black bladed saber in the other. The skull's eye holes no longer glowed red, and its jaw broke off and fell into the water. Arvek himself looked a little beat up. His long black hair was messy, he was bleeding from a gash on his cheek, and his long leather coat was singed and torn in several places. If he'd just beat the zombie dragon, how could I possibly hope to survive this?

I scrambled backward, slipping in the mud and falling onto my butt where I continued scooting away.

Arvek dropped the dragon skull into the water and sloshed toward me.

I pulled out my remaining dagger and held it up in front of me as I carefully stood. "Stay back!"

Arvek laughed and in a blur of motion rushed forward swinging his saber. I raised my knife but Arvek sliced the blade from the hilt. I looked down at the broken dagger and dropped it.

Arvek shook his head. "You have no idea what you've gotten yourself into." Then he backhanded me and the world spun. When it stopped, I found myself lying in the mud, blood running from my nose.

"Pathetic," Arvek sneered. "I cannot imagine why my master would warn me to be careful of you." Arvek grabbed me by the collar of my shirt and forced me to stand. "You are nothing!"

All my years of stranger-danger training suddenly came back to me, and I kicked Arvek as hard as I could in the crotch. He stumbled backward, sucking in a gasp as he doubled over, and I took the opportunity to run. I didn't know where I'd go, or how'd I get out of the gully, but I didn't care. I just ran.

But it didn't matter. Arvek appeared in front of me faster than I could stop, and I ran right into his fist. I saw a flash of light behind my eyelids and then I was on the ground. I rolled onto my back, coughing as I choked on blood from my nose. I opened my eyes to find a gloved hand gripping my throat. Arvek effortlessly lifted me from the ground by the neck and raised me in the air so my feet dangled inches off the ground. He squeezed, and my vision began to darken. Just before I passed out, he dropped me to the ground. I gasped for air, but didn't get much before Arvek kicked me hard in the ribs.

I tried to teleport again, but it still felt like flexing a sore muscle. Arvek stepped around me, poking lightly at my pocket with the point of his saber. "My master ordered that I bring you to him alive, so that you could give the crystal directly to him. I guess he doesn't trust even his most devoted servants to not try and take it for themselves."

I was finally able to keep some of my air and was on the way to breathing normally again.

"To be honest, it hurts my feelings," Arvek said.

There was something in Arvek's voice that made my chest tighten.

Arvek gently cut open my pocket and the blue glow of the Crystal of Time lit up the ground.

"Do you know what we Dreja prize over all other things, Thomas?"

I'd managed to look up at him, and I really didn't like the look on his face. It looked hungry, and not in the good *it's time for pizza* way.

"Power, Thomas," Arvek said. "It means more to us than any loyalty or oath. It's really the only thing we respect."

He's going to kill me and take the crystal for himself!

I rolled away, and crawled toward the water. I'm not sure why I picked that direction, but it really didn't matter. I had scarcely reached the muddy bank when Arvek grabbed the back of my shirt, lifted me from the ground, and tossed me into the shallows.

The crystal fell from my pocket and sank to the bottom of the pond's shallow edge. Arvek reached into the water to grab it, but the crystal flashed, and he drew his hand back with a hiss. I rose up out of the water, watching Arvek examine his fingers. The crystal had actually burned away two fingers of Arvek's black leather glove. He looked at me, smiled, and then charged.

I ran, but slipped and fell into the water. When I tried to rise again, Arvek slammed me in the back of the head and forced my face under water. He held me there past when my lungs started to burn, and panic made my thoughts slippery. He let go, and I lifted my head up, gasping and choking.

Arvek leaned in close to my ear and hissed, "You are never going home!"

He shoved my head back under water, and this time I knew he wouldn't let me up. This was it. This was the end. Mom would grow old and die, and there wouldn't even be an older version of myself to visit her grave, like I saw in the scene Adrayen showed me. I had made a mess of everything. Darius would die, and Bruno would be stuck here forever if Arvek didn't just kill him and the others. Worst of all,

Adrayen would be one step closer to becoming a god—all because I was a coward.

Bubbles escaped my mouth and I breathed in water.

But I hadn't been a coward, something whispered to me. After I summoned Arvek, I chose to fight him and not give Adrayen the crystal. I chose to side with the guardians even though it meant I couldn't go home. It might've come a little late, but I had *sacrificed* for the greater good.

Light exploded before my eyes and the Hero Blade was in my hand. As soon as my wet skin touched its handle I felt strength flow into me. I swung the Hero Blade up and out of the water while at the same time rolling to the side. Arvek screamed as the hand he'd been using to push my head under flew free of his wrist. I exploded up in a spray of water and rammed the Hero Blade forward as hard as I could, piercing Arvek through the heart.

His mouth fell open, and his eyes rolled down to look at the sword that was sprouting out of his chest. He slowly fell backward, his weight forcing the blade of the sword down so he slid off of it and collapsed into the mud, dead.

Arvek was dead, and I had killed him.

24

LOBO'S SON

I climbed out of the gully and ran back the way I'd come. The trees surrounding the area were black and smoldering, but no longer on fire. The headless skeleton of Olis's zombie dragon lay in pieces all over the ground in front of the temple. Even though it was destroyed, I still avoided running too close to its bones. I mean, if it can come back once, right?

When I entered the temple, I was met by the sight of Dreja mutant bodies lying all across the marble floor, pools of green blood oozing out from underneath some of them. They were all dead or dying. Incredibly, Bruno, the druid, and the green dude had successfully defeated them all and won the day. I saw the three crowded at the base of the grand staircase surrounding Darius, who lay in the same spot I'd left him. For some reason, the druid was kneeling on the ground, the green dude once again separate and in his normal form with wide brimmed black hat and sunglasses. I ran to them.

"Darius?" I shouted.

"Thomas!" A scraped and bruised Bruno tried to hug me, but I dodged away and fell to my knees at Darius's side. He was still breathing, but had turned white, and was grimacing. I met the druid's eyes, and for once the man looked genuinely concerned.

"He's bleeding out from the stomach." The druid shook his head. "I tried to stop it, but Arvek's sword was enchanted to leave cursed wounds that won't stop bleeding." The druid bowed his head, suddenly looking ashamed. "I'm sorry. I can't help with stuff like this anymore."

What did that mean?

"Thomas," Darius said. His weak voice scared me.

"It's ok, Darius. Arvek's dead, and we need to get you off this island and find help."

Darius didn't reply immediately, but instead eyed the Hero Blade that I'd sheathed in my belt. He smiled. "You have become a hero."

I shook my head, tears running down my cheeks. "I betrayed you! It's because of me that you're..."

"Dying?" Darius finished.

I nodded, sniffing and wiping my nose on my wet sleeve. "Let's go!" I said and made to lift Darius from the floor.

"No," Darius said.

"We need to get you help!"

Darius slowly shook his head. "The nearest help is weeks away. I won't survive that long."

"Then take the crystal." I pulled the glowing shard from my other pocket, the one Arvek hadn't torn open. "Its magic can help you until we..."

"Thomas," Darius cut me off. "It's too late. The crystal

can't save me now."

Those words fell on me like a snowy avalanche. Darius was going to die, and it was my fault.

"Darius, I'm so sorry. I didn't mean for any of this to happen," I sobbed.

"Listen Thomas!" Darius ordered, something that sounded strange in his weak voice. "Remember how I told you my father looked into the future and afterward told me I would someday save the universe from Adrayen?"

I nodded.

Darius coughed. "What father actually said was *my son* would save the universe from Adrayen." Darius gripped my forearm and stared into my face. "I thought he was talking about me, but I was wrong."

"But you're his son," I said, and now I was really confused.

"Not his only son," Darius said.

It was like my heart just stopped, and I stared stupidly down at Darius's pale face. Could it really be true? Did I even want it to be true?

"Yes," he wheezed. "You're my little brother."

"But how?"

"Well, Thomas," Bruno said. "When a mommy bird and a daddy bee really love each other..."

I waved for Bruno to be quiet and he stopped.

"It was you that father saw. That's why he sought you out. I think he was going to start training you to be the next Destiny Keeper."

"No." I shook my head. "That can't be right."

"It's true. My mother died fourteen years ago when our

world was destroyed. I was hidden by the other guardians, and so father went away to grieve and figure things out. He must've gone to Earth where he met your mother."

"But why did he abandon us?"

Darius closed his eyes and swallowed. "I don't know. And I don't know how he transferred the bond to you before you touched the crystal. All I know is that *you* must be the one to fulfill Kaylor's prophecy, not me."

"I'm not a Destiny Keeper!"

"Maybe not yet," Darius choked. "But you can be."

I bowed my head, spilling my tears onto the stone floor. "I betrayed you."

"Part of that is my fault. I should've told you everything when we first met. It's just that," he coughed. "I was jealous that father had given you the bond, and worried that it meant he wanted you to be the next Destiny Keeper instead of me. I shouldn't have treated you like competition. I should've been your friend."

"You are," I sobbed.

Darius grimaced in pain for a moment before continuing. "I don't have much time, so no more interrupting!"

I nodded, trying to steady my breathing and stop the tears. It didn't work.

"In my things is a map of Iskarin. Use it to find a way back to the Crossroads. Don't go back the way we came, or use the same gate. Adrayen will expect that." Darius gritted his teeth, his voice straining for a moment. "And watch out for Olis. He's not going to give up trying to get the crystal from you, especially now that you have it."

I almost told him about the bone-dragon, but I didn't.

Time was too short.

"After you get back, try to find a guardian spy. There are a few left watching the Crossroads. That's your best chance for finding where Drake is hiding out. Go to Drake. He is a powerful magician and can teach you how to fight. Together you can make our last stand against Adrayen and his Dreja armies."

I shook my head. "Darius, I can't do this. I'm just a kid!"

Darius reached up and grabbed the front of my wet scout shirt and used it to pull me closer so he could look me in the eyes. "You-have-to!"

"But I'm nobody," I protested.

Darius let go of my shirt. "You killed one of Adrayen's four lieutenants. That's something no guardian has done in centuries."

"I got lucky."

Darius smiled and said, "There's no such thing as luck. You defeated him by the strength of your will."

"Darius," I sobbed.

"Will-is-everything," Darius choked on his words as blood bubbled from his mouth. "We have-the-power-to decide-our-own-fate," Darius coughed. "Your-will-is-your-greatest-weapon."

"Darius!" I shook him, but it didn't help. He was fading.

"Will-is..." and that was all that came out of his mouth before he exhaled a final breath and grew still.

After what seemed like an eternity of walking down the temple stairs, we finally reached the catacombs. Without Darius's light spell, I had to light a lantern so we could see in the dark of the basement. After that, we walked steadily down the narrow corridor, Bruno blubbering something I couldn't understand as he carried Darius's lifeless body in his arms—my brother's body. That still hadn't sunk in. *I actually have an older brother, or had*, I thought.

The green dude gibbered something that sounded sad, and the druid was unusually silent. When we reached the end of the long hallway, I had the druid help me remove the stone lid. We removed its treasures, and Bruno laid Darius's body in the coffin. I stared at Darius's face. His eyes were closed, and we folded his hands across his chest. I smoothed some of his long black hair out of his face, and when I was done it just looked like he was sleeping.

We replaced the stone lid and I felt like I should've said some words, but each time I tried I either couldn't think of anything or I started sobbing. In the end, we just gave him a respectful silence and left.

Everyone stayed quiet as we left the temple ruins and made our way back through the dense jungle. When we reached the island's rocky shore, I found Norman the boatman patiently waiting. He wasn't wearing his cloak anymore, revealing a muscled and twisted red body similar to that of Arvek's Dreja mutants. The cloak—which Bruno had vomited on only hours earlier—was wet and hung over the side of the boat to dry. Norman glared at Bruno as we climbed down onto the boat. Then he launched the craft into the water and started sailing us back toward the mainland.

On the way back, the mood of the others lightened, and I heard them begin to talk about the battle we'd just won. The druid, of course, claimed to have defeated fifty-seven Dreja mutants by himself, though I'd only counted fifteen total.

The green dude gibbered something that sounded like he was disputing the druid's claim, and Bruno bemoaned the fact that he'd missed an opportunity to taste Dreja mutant meat. That sparked a discussion on what Dreja mutant meat would taste like, Bruno and the druid finally agreeing that it must taste like Dreja mutant chicken.

It made me smile, which I really needed at the moment.

We finally made it back to the mainland and Norman waited quietly for us to disembark. Afterwards we stood on the beach watching Norman's craft sail away and disappear into a magical cloud of mist.

"Bye Nathan!" Bruno shouted as he waved his arms.

I stared after Norman until the creature and his boat disappeared completely. Then I reached into my good pocket and pulled out the Crystal of Time. I stared into it, wondering if I could look into the future and find out more about what I was supposed to do.

Nothing happened.

I sighed, put the crystal back in my pocket and turned to find the others staring at me. They looked like they were waiting for me to say something.

"I'm going to try to find Drake, like Darius wanted."

They just continued to stare.

"That means we won't be going home," I said to Bruno. "It also means that Adrayen will be coming after us," I said after turning to face the druid. "I'll understand if any of you want to go your own way," I finished by looking at the green dude.

A long moment passed without anyone saying anything, and then Bruno broke the silence by lunging forward and scooping me up into another bone-crunching bear hug. "I'll always help you, Thomas!" He set me down and let me go.

"Thanks, Bruno," I wheezed.

The druid shrugged. "Eh. I've got nothing better to do."

I looked at the gelatinous, green, sunglasses-and-black-hat-wearing creature we'd named the green dude. It jabbered something that sounded excited.

"I have no idea what you're saying," I said. "But I'll assume you're coming with us?"

The green dude gibbered a reply that was either agreement or a recipe for frosted bran muffins—I'm not sure.

"Where do we go now?" Bruno asked.

"To find another way back to the Crossroads," I said.

"I shall guide you to find this elusive portal!" The druid said dramatically.

"No offense, Druid, but I'd rather go back to Zombieville and let the undead feast on my entrails."

"Please," the druid begged. "I promise to keep the lies to a minimum."

I shook my head. "I think *this time* I'll use a map." I pulled out Darius's map, unrolled it and found the Sea of Ages. After a minute, I picked a direction, rolled the map and started walking. The others followed me, and I couldn't help from repeatedly glancing at the sky, worried that another zombie-dragon might be flying around looking for us.

After walking the beach for an hour without any bone dragon attacks, I relaxed and started thinking about Mom and home. It hurt to know that I might never make it back, or see her again, but I knew I was doing the right thing. I wanted so badly to tell her what I found out about my dad, and how there was probably a good reason he'd left us, but that only made me want to cry. That's when the crystal showed me another vision.

I saw myself walking up to my front door. I was dressed in a tunic and still wore my scout pants, and Lobo's Hero Blade was belted in a sheath at my side. I was a little taller and my face was dirty, but otherwise I looked the same as I did now. I was alone, no Bruno, druid, or green dude following me.

I saw my future-self step up onto my front porch, hesitate, and then knock on the door. After a moment, it opened up part way to reveal Mom's face. When she saw me she froze, leaving the door mostly closed. She stared at me for a long time and then threw open the door, and hugged me. We were both crying.

The vision ended and I found myself blinking away tears. I had just seen the future. Not a warning of something bad about to happen, but of what I hoped would be the end of my journey. I had no idea how far into the future I saw, but I was sure it *was* the future. I would go home someday! And not when I'm an old man and Mom is dead. I would go home! It was my destiny!

I laughed out loud.

"Are you ok, Thomas?" Bruno asked.

I smiled at him. "I will be."

"Mind sickness," the druid whispered to Bruno. "Good thing I'm a licensed exorcist."

"Druid!" I snapped. "What did we say about the lies?"

"Oh, you were serious? Come on, just one more?!"

I shook my head, still smiling.

ACKNOWLEDGMENTS

Thanks goes to Amanda Wintch, Zach Bjorge, Riley Horn, Stoney Beckstead, Adam Boswell, James Wymore, Bryce Wilson, Holli Anderson, Miranda Roberts-Moore, David West, Christina King, Samuel King, Rebekah King, and Curiosity Quills Press.

ABOUT THE AUTHOR

For years Jason King publicly proclaimed his identity as "the chosen one," but medication and a stint in a minimum security health and wellness facility convinced him that was not the case. In order to cope with his greatly diminished role in society, he devoted his free time to making up stories. He's the author of The Age of the Infinite Trilogy, and Valcoria Children of the Crystal Star from Curiosity Quills Press.

Born in Salt Lake City Utah, Jason grew up on a steady diet of anime, science fiction, Dungeons and Dragons, JRPG's, and chocolate cake donuts. By some inexplicable cosmic anomaly Jason managed to marry, and is the proud father of four children, one of which is certainly destined to one day slay him and absorb his soul.

Jason holds a bachelor's degree in I.T. Management and is currently the Internet Marketing Manager for a local bookstore chain. He's the author of The Age of the Infinite Trilogy, and Valcoria Children of the Crystal Star from Curiosity Quills Press. He is also a proud "anonymous"

member of the Space Balrogs comedy troupe, and he speaks
fluent Labrador.

ABOUT THE AUTHOR

Born and raised in the slums of ancient Mesopotamia during the Bronze Age (Salt Lake City in 1979, according to his birth certificate), Jon Grundvig overcame these imagined obstacles to become - in his own inaccurate and self-aggrandizing words - a general, an astronaut, an Olympic gold medalist, and the greatest Flamenco dancer Madrid has ever seen. He also claims to be - despite a mountain of genealogical evidence to the contrary - a direct descendant of Ghengis Khan.

When his lifelong dream of being a masked knife fighter in the streets of Tijuana fizzled, Jon turned to writing, acting, and other creative ventures as part of his court ordered community service. Due to his own former experience as a robed forest shaman (or his constant, pathological lying, depending on who you ask) the character of The Druid was based in part on Grundvig's persona.

Until he can break free from the oppressive shackles of office cubicle life and find another way to pay off his crippling gambling debts, Jon currently works as an inventory analyst for a local furniture retail chain. He dreams of one day running off with his wife and 3 sons and retiring to an exciting life of piracy on the open seas. Rumors that he has a secret second family hidden somewhere in the mountains could not be substantiated.